Hertfordshire

2 6 OCT 2007
10th Jan 11
Shear 2/17

BUS

Please renew/return this item by the last date shown.

| From Area codes 01923 or 020: | From Area codes of Herts: |
|---|---|
| Renewals: 01923 471373 | 01438 737373 |
| Enquiries: 01923 471333 | 01438 737333 |
| Textphone: 01923 471599 | 01438 737599 |

www.herts

D1421461

H45 267 880 8

# F. SCOTT FITZGERALD

# Magnetism

GREAT LOVES

PENGUIN BOOKS

Published by the Penguin Group
Penguin Books Ltd, 80 Strand, London WC2R ORL, England
Penguin Group (USA) Inc., 375 Hudson Street, New York, New York 10014, USA
Penguin Group (Canada), 90 Eglinton Avenue East, Suite 700, Toronto, Ontario, Canada M4P 2Y3
(a division of Pearson Penguin Canada Inc.)
Penguin Ireland, 25 St Stephen's Green, Dublin 2, Ireland
(a division of Penguin Books Ltd)
Penguin Group (Australia), 250 Camberwell Road, Camberwell, Victoria 3124, Australia
(a division of Pearson Australia Group Pty Ltd)
Penguin Books India Pvt Ltd, 11 Community Centre, Panchsheel Park, New Delhi – 110 017, India
Penguin Group (NZ), 67 Apollo Drive, Rosedale, North Shore 0632, New Zealand
(a division of Pearson New Zealand Ltd)
Penguin Books (South Africa) (Pty) Ltd, 24 Sturdee Avenue,
Rosebank, Johannesburg 2196, South Africa

Penguin Books Ltd, Registered Offices: 80 Strand, London WC2R ORL, England

www.penguin.com

*The Collected Short Stories* first published 1986
This selection published in Penguin Books 2007

1

Typeset by Rowland Phototypesetting Ltd, Bury St Edmunds, Suffolk
Printed in England by Clays Ltd, St Ives plc

978–0–141–03287–0

# Contents

F. Scott Fitzgerald (1896–1940) was born in St Paul, Minnesota. He was said to have epitomized the Jazz Age, which he himself defined as 'a generation grown up to find all Gods dead, all wars fought, all faiths in man shaken'. In 1920 he married Zelda Sayre. Their traumatic marriage and subsequent breakdowns became the leading influence in his writing. Among his publications were five novels, *This Side of Paradise*, *The Great Gatsby*, *The Beautiful and the Damned*, *Tender is the Night* and *The Last Tycoon* (his last and unfinished work); six volumes of short stories and *The Crack-Up*, a selection of autobiographical pieces.

# 'The Sensible Thing'

## I

At the Great American Lunch Hour young George O'Kelly straightened his desk deliberately and with an assumed air of interest. No one in the office must know that he was in a hurry, for success is a matter of atmosphere, and it is not well to advertise the fact that your mind is separated from your work by a distance of seven hundred miles.

But once out of the building he set his teeth and began to run, glancing now and then at the gay noon of early spring which filled Times Square and loitered less than twenty feet over the heads of the crowd. The crowd all looked slightly upwards and took deep March breaths, and the sun dazzled their eyes so that scarcely anyone saw anyone else but only their own reflection on the sky.

George O'Kelly, whose mind was over seven hundred miles away, thought that all outdoors was horrible. He rushed into the subway, and for ninety-five blocks bent a frenzied glance on a car-card which showed vividly how he had only one chance in five of keeping his teeth for ten years. At 137th Street he broke off his study of commercial art, left the subway, and began to run again, a tireless, anxious run that brought him this time to his home – one room in a high, horrible apartment-house in the middle of nowhere.

There it was on the bureau, the letter – in sacred ink, on blessed paper – all over the city, people, if they listened, could hear the beating of George O'Kelly's heart. He read the commas, the blots, and the thumb-smudge on the margin – then he threw himself hopelessly upon his bed.

He was in a mess, one of those terrific messes which are ordinary incidents in the life of the poor, which follow poverty like birds of prey. The poor go under or go up or go wrong or even go on, somehow, in a way the poor have – but George O'Kelly was so new to poverty that had any one denied the uniqueness of his case he would have been astounded.

Less than two years ago he had been graduated with honours from the Massachusetts Institute of Technology and had taken a position with a firm of construction engineers in southern Tennessee. All his life he had thought in terms of tunnels and skyscrapers and great squat dams and tall, three-towered bridges, that were like dancers holding hands in a row, with heads as tall as cities and skirts of cable strand. It had seemed romantic to George O'Kelly to change the sweep of rivers and the shape of mountains so that life could flourish in the old bad lands of the world where it had never taken root before. He loved steel, and there was always steel near him in his dreams, liquid steel, steel in bars, and blocks and beams and formless plastic masses, waiting for him, as paint and canvas to his hand. Steel inexhaustible, to be made lovely and austere in his imaginative fire . . .

At present he was an insurance clerk at forty dollars a week with his dream slipping fast behind him. The dark little girl who had made this mess, this terrible and intolerable mess, was waiting to be sent for in a town in Tennessee.

In fifteen minutes the woman from whom he sublet his room knocked and asked him with maddening kindness if, since he was home, he would have some lunch. He shook his head, but the interruption aroused him, and getting up from the bed he wrote a telegram.

'Letter depressed me have you lost your nerve you are foolish and just upset to think of breaking off why not marry me immediately sure we can make it all right –'

He hesitated for a wild minute, and then added in a hand that could scarcely be recognized as his own: 'In any case I will arrive tomorrow at six o'clock.'

When he finished he ran out of the apartment and down to the telegraph office near the subway stop. He possessed in this world not quite one hundred dollars, but the letter showed that she was 'nervous' and this left him no choice. He knew what 'nervous' meant – that she was emotionally depressed, that the prospect of marrying into a life of poverty and struggle was putting too much strain upon her love.

George O'Kelly reached the insurance company at his usual run, the run that had become almost second nature to him, that seemed best to express the tension under which he lived. He went straight to the manager's office.

'I want to see you, Mr Chambers,' he announced breathlessly.

'Well?' Two eyes, eyes like winter windows, glared at him with ruthless impersonality.

'I want to get four days' vacation.'

'Why, you had a vacation just two weeks ago!' said Mr Chambers in surprise.

'That's true,' admitted the distraught young man, 'but now I've got to have another.'

'Where'd you go last time? To your home?'

'No, I went to – a place in Tennessee.'

'Well, where do you want to go this time?'

'Well, this time I want to go to – a place in Tennessee.'

'You're consistent, anyhow,' said the manager dryly. 'But I didn't realize you were employed here as a travelling salesman.'

'I'm not,' cried George desperately, 'but I've got to go.'

'All right,' agreed Mr Chambers, 'but you don't have to come back. So don't!'

'I won't.' And to his own astonishment as well as Mr Chambers' George's face grew pink with pleasure. He felt happy, exultant – for the first time in six months he was absolutely free. Tears of gratitude stood in his eyes, and he seized Mr Chambers warmly by the hand.

'I want to thank you,' he said with a rush of emotion, 'I don't want to come back. I think I'd have gone crazy if you'd said that I could come back. Only I couldn't quit myself, you see, and I want to thank you for – for quitting for me.'

He waved his hand magnanimously, shouted aloud, 'You owe me three days' salary but you can keep it!' and rushed from the office. Mr Chambers rang for his stenographer to ask if O'Kelly had seemed queer lately. He had fired many men in the course of his career, and they had taken it in many different ways, but none of them had thanked him – ever before.

## II

Jonquil Cary was her name, and to George O'Kelly nothing had ever looked so fresh and pale as her face when she saw him and fled to him eagerly along the station platform. Her arms were raised to him, her mouth was half parted for his kiss, when she held him off suddenly and lightly and, with a touch of embarrassment, looked around. Two boys, somewhat younger than George, were standing in the background.

'This is Mr Craddock and Mr Holt,' she announced cheerfully. 'You met them when you were here before.'

Disturbed by the transition of a kiss into an introduction and suspecting some hidden significance, George was more confused when he found that the automobile which was to carry them to Jonquil's house belonged to one of the two young men. It seemed to put him at a disadvantage. On the way Jonquil chattered between the front and back seats, and when he tried to slip his arm around her under cover of the twilight she compelled him with a quick movement to take her hand instead.

...is street on the way to your house?' he whis-
...d. 'I don't recognize it.'

'It's the new boulevard. Jerry just got this car today,
and he wants to show it to me before he takes us
home.'

When, after twenty minutes, they were deposited at
Jonquil's house, George felt that the first happiness of
the meeting, the joy he had recognized so surely in her
eyes back in the station, had been dissipated by the
intrusion of the ride. Something that he had looked
forward to had been rather casually lost, and he was
brooding on this as he said good night stiffly to the
two young men. Then his ill-humour faded as Jonquil
drew him into a familiar embrace under the dim light
of the front hall and told him in a dozen ways, of which
the best was without words, how she had missed him.
Her emotion reassured him, promised his anxious heart
that everything would be all right.

They sat together on the sofa, overcome by each
other's presence, beyond all except fragmentary endear-
ments. At the supper hour Jonquil's father and mother
appeared and were glad to see George. They liked him,
and had been interested in his engineering career when
he had first come to Tennessee over a year before. They
had been sorry when he had given it up and gone to
New York to look for something more immediately
profitable, but while they deplored the curtailment of
his career they sympathized with him and were ready to
recognize the engagement. During dinner they asked
about his progress in New York.

'Everything's going fine,' he told them with enthusiasm. 'I've been promoted – better salary.'

He was miserable as he said this – but they were all so glad.

'They must like you,' said Mrs Cary, 'that's certain – or they wouldn't let you off twice in three weeks to come down here.'

'I told them they had to,' explained George hastily; 'I told them if they didn't I wouldn't work for them any more.'

'But you ought to save your money,' Mrs Cary reproached him gently. 'Not spend it all on this expensive trip.'

Dinner was over – he and Jonquil were alone and she came back into his arms.

'So glad you're here,' she sighed. 'Wish you never were going away again, darling.'

'Do you miss me?'

'Oh, so much, so much.'

'Do you – do other men come to see you often? Like those two kids?'

The question surprised her. The dark velvet eyes stared at him.

'Why, of course they do. All the time. Why – I've told you in letters that they did, dearest.'

This was true – when he had first come to the city there had been already a dozen boys around her, responding to her picturesque fragility with adolescent worship, and a few of them perceiving that her beautiful eyes were also sane and kind.

'Do you expect me never to go anywhere' – Jonquil demanded, leaning back against the sofa-pillows until she seemed to look at him from many miles away – 'and just fold my hands and sit still – forever?'

'What do you mean?' he blurted out in a panic. 'Do you mean you think I'll never have enough money to marry you?'

'Oh, don't jump at conclusions so, George.'

'I'm not jumping at conclusions. That's what you said.'

George decided suddenly that he was on dangerous grounds. He had not intended to let anything spoil this night. He tried to take her again in his arms, but she resisted unexpectedly, saying:

'It's hot. I'm going to get the electric fan.'

When the fan was adjusted they sat down again, but he was in a supersensitive mood and involuntarily he plunged into the specific world he had intended to avoid.

'When will you marry me?'

'Are you ready for me to marry you?'

All at once his nerves gave way, and he sprang to his feet.

'Let's shut off that damned fan,' he cried, 'it drives me wild. It's like a clock ticking away all the time I'll be with you. I came here to be happy and forget everything about New York and time –'

He sank down on the sofa as suddenly as he had risen. Jonquil turned off the fan, and drawing his head down into her lap began stroking his hair.

'Let's sit like this,' she said softly, 'just sit quiet

like this, and I'll put you to sleep. You're all tired and nervous and your sweetheart'll take care of you.'

'But I don't want to sit like this,' he complained, jerking up suddenly, 'I don't want to sit like this at all. I want you to kiss me. That's the only thing that makes me rest. And any ways I'm not nervous – it's you that's nervous. I'm not nervous at all.'

To prove that he wasn't nervous he left the couch and plumped himself into a rocking-chair across the room.

'Just when I'm ready to marry you you write me the most nervous letters, as if you're going to back out, and I have to come rushing down here –'

'You don't have to come if you don't want to.'

'But I *do* want to!' insisted George.

It seemed to him that he was being very cool and logical and that she was putting him deliberately in the wrong. With every word they were drawing farther and farther apart – and he was unable to stop himself or to keep worry and pain out of his voice.

But in a minute Jonquil began to cry sorrowfully and he came back to the sofa and put his arm around her. He was the comforter now, drawing her head close to his shoulder, murmuring old familiar things until she grew calmer and only trembled a little, spasmodically, in his arms. For over an hour they sat there, while the evening pianos thumped their last cadences into the street outside. George did not move, or think, or hope, lulled into numbness by the premonition of disaster. The clock would tick on, past eleven, past twelve, and then Mrs Cary would call down gently over the banister – beyond that he saw only tomorrow and despair.

## III

In the heat of the next day the breaking-point came. They had each guessed the truth about the other, but of the two she was the more ready to admit the situation.

'There's no use going on,' she said miserably, 'you know you hate the insurance business, and you'll never do well in it.'

'That's not it,' he insisted stubbornly; 'I hate going on alone. If you'll marry me and come with me and take a chance with me, I can make good at anything, but not while I'm worrying about you down here.'

She was silent a long time before she answered, not thinking – for she had seen the end – but only waiting, because she knew that every word would seem more cruel than the last. Finally she spoke:

'George, I love you with all my heart, and I don't see how I can ever love anyone else but you. If you'd been ready for me two months ago I'd have married you – now I can't because it doesn't seem to be the sensible thing.'

He made wild accusations – there was someone else – she was keeping something from him!

'No, there's no one else.'

This was true. But reacting from the strain of this affair she had found relief in the company of young boys like Jerry Holt, who had the merit of meaning absolutely nothing in her life.

George didn't take the situation well, at all. He seized her in his arms and tried literally to kiss her into marrying him at once. When this failed, he broke into a long monologue of self-pity, and ceased only when he saw that he was making himself despicable in her sight. He threatened to leave when he had no intention of leaving, and refused to go when she told him that, after all, it was best that he should.

For a while she was sorry, then for another while she was merely kind.

'You'd better go now,' she cried at last, so loud that Mrs Cary came downstairs in alarm.

'Is something the matter?'

'I'm going away, Mrs Cary,' said George brokenly. Jonquil had left the room.

'Don't feel so badly, George.' Mrs Cary blinked at him in helpless sympathy – sorry and, in the same breath, glad that the little tragedy was almost done. 'If I were you I'd go home to your mother for a week or so. Perhaps after all this is the sensible thing –'

'Please don't talk,' he cried. 'Please don't say anything to me now!'

Jonquil came into the room again, her sorrow and her nervousness alike tucked under powder and rouge and hat.

'I've ordered a taxicab,' she said impersonally. 'We can drive around until your train leaves.'

She walked out on the front porch. George put on his coat and hat and stood for a minute exhausted in the hall – he had eaten scarcely a bite since he had left New York. Mrs Cary came over, drew his head down and kissed him on the cheek, and he felt very ridiculous and weak in his knowledge that the scene had been ridiculous and weak at the end. If he had only gone the night before – left her for the last time with a decent pride.

The taxi had come, and for an hour these two that had been lovers rode along the less-frequented streets. He held her hand and grew calmer in the sunshine, seeing too late that there had been nothing all along to do or say.

'I'll come back,' he told her.

'I know you will,' she answered, trying to put a cheery faith into her voice. 'And we'll write each other – sometimes.'

'No,' he said, 'we won't write. I couldn't stand that. Some day I'll come back.'

'I'll never forget you, George.'

They reached the station, and she went with him while he bought his ticket . . .

'Why, George O'Kelly and Jonquil Cary!'

It was a man and a girl whom George had known when he had worked in town, and Jonquil seemed to greet their presence with relief. For an interminable five minutes they all stood there talking; then the train roared into the station, and with ill-concealed agony in his face George held out his arms towards Jonquil. She took an uncertain step towards him, faltered, and then pressed his hand quickly as if she were taking leave of a chance friend.

'Good-bye, George,' she was saying, 'I hope you have a pleasant trip.

'Good-bye, George. Come back and see us all again.'

Dumb, almost blind with pain, he seized his suitcase,

and in some dazed way got himself aboard the train.

Past clanging street-crossings, gathering speed through wide suburban spaces towards the sunset. Perhaps she too would see the sunset and pause for a moment, turning, remembering, before he faded with her sleep into the past. This night's dusk would cover up forever the sun and the trees and the flowers and laughter of his young world.

## IV

On a damp afternoon in September of the following year a young man with his face burned to a deep copper glow got off a train at a city in Tennessee. He looked around anxiously, and seemed relieved when he found that there was no one in the station to meet him. He taxied to the best hotel in the city where he registered with some satisfaction as George O'Kelly, Cuzco, Peru.

Up in his room he sat for a few minutes at the window looking down into the familiar street below. Then with his hand trembling faintly he took off the telephone receiver and called a number.

'Is Miss Jonquil in?'

'This is she.'

'Oh –' His voice after overcoming a faint tendency to waver went on with friendly formality.

'This is George O'Kelly. Did you get my letter?'

'Yes. I thought you'd be in today.'

Her voice, cool and unmoved, disturbed him, but not as he had expected. This was the voice of a stranger, unexcited, pleasantly glad to see him – that was all. He wanted to put down the telephone and catch his breath.

'I haven't seen you for – a long time.' He succeeded in making this sound offhand. 'Over a year.'

He knew how long it had been – to the day.

'It'll be awfully nice to talk to you again.'

'I'll be there in about an hour.'

He hung up. For four long seasons every minute of his leisure had been crowded with anticipation of this hour, and now this hour was here. He had thought of finding her married, engaged, in love – he had not thought she would be unstirred at his return.

There would never again in his life, he felt, be another ten months like these he had just gone through. He had made an admittedly remarkable showing for a young engineer – stumbled into two unusual opportunities, one in Peru, whence he had just returned, and another consequent upon it, in New York, whither he was bound. In this short time he had risen from poverty into a position of unlimited opportunity.

He looked at himself in the dressing-table mirror. He was almost black with tan, but it was a romantic black, and in the last week, since he had had time to think it, it had given him considerable pleasure. The hardiness of his frame, too, he appraised with a sort of fascination. He had lost part of an eyebrow somewhere, and he still wore an elastic bandage on his knee, but he was too young not to realize that on the steamer many women had looked at him with unusual tributary interest.

His clothes, of course, were frightful. They had been

made for him by a Greek tailor in Lima – in two days. He was young enough, too, to have explained this sartorial deficiency to Jonquil in his otherwise laconic note. The only further detail it contained was a request that he should *not* be met at the station.

George O'Kelly, of Cuzco, Peru, waited an hour and a half in the hotel, until, to be exact, the sun had reached a midway position in the sky. Then, freshly shaven and talcum-powdered towards a somewhat more Caucasian hue, for vanity at the last minute had overcome romance, he engaged a taxicab and set out for the house he knew so well.

He was breathing hard – he noticed this but he told himself that it was excitement, not emotion. He was here; she was not married – that was enough. He was not even sure what he had to say to her. But this was the moment of his life that he felt he could least easily have dispensed with. There was no triumph, after all, without a girl concerned, and if he did not lay his spoils at her feet he could at least hold them for a passing moment before her eyes.

The house loomed up suddenly beside him, and his first thought was that it had assumed a strange un-reality. There was nothing changed – only everything was changed. It was smaller and it seemed shabbier than before – there was no cloud of magic hovering over its roof and issuing from the windows of the upper floor. He rang the doorbell and an unfamiliar coloured maid appeared. Miss Jonquil would be down in a moment. He wet his lips nervously and walked into the sitting-room – and the feeling of unreality increased. After all, he saw, this was only a room, and not the enchanted chamber where he had passed those poignant hours. He sat in a chair, amazed to find it a chair, realizing that his imagination had distorted and coloured all these simple familiar things.

Then the door opened and Jonquil came into the room – and it was as though everything in it suddenly blurred before his eyes. He had not remembered how beautiful she was, and he felt his face grow pale and his voice diminish to a poor sigh in his throat.

She was dressed in pale green, and a gold ribbon bound back her dark, straight hair like a crown. The familiar velvet eyes caught his as she came through the door, and a spasm of fright went through him at her beauty's power of inflicting pain.

He said 'Hello', and they each took a few steps forward and shook hands. Then they sat in chairs quite far apart and gazed at each other across the room.

'You've come back,' she said, and he answered just as tritely: 'I wanted to stop in and see you as I came through.'

He tried to neutralize the tremor in his voice by looking anywhere but at her face. The obligation to speak was on him, but, unless he immediately began to boast, it seemed that there was nothing to say. There had never been anything casual in their previous relations – it didn't seem possible that people in this position would talk about the weather.

'This is ridiculous,' he broke out in sudden embarrassment. 'I don't know exactly what to do. Does my being here bother you?'

'No.' The answer was both reticent and impersonally sad. It depressed him.

'Are you engaged?' he demanded.

'No.'

'Are you in love with someone?'

She shook her head.

'Oh.' He leaned back in his chair. Another subject seemed exhausted – the interview was not taking the course he had intended.

'Jonquil,' he began, this time on a softer key, 'after all that's happened between us, I wanted to come back and see you. Whatever I do in the future I'll never love another girl as I've loved you.'

This was one of the speeches he had rehearsed. On the steamer it had seemed to have just the right note – a reference to the tenderness he would always feel for her combined with a non-committal attitude towards his present state of mind. Here with the past around him, beside him, growing minute by minute more heavy on the air, it seemed theatrical and stale.

She made no comment, sat without moving, her eyes fixed on him with an expression that might have meant everything or nothing.

'You don't love me any more, do you?' he asked her in a level voice.

'No.'

When Mrs Cary came in a minute later, and spoke to him about his success – there had been a half-column about him in the local paper – he was a mixture of emotions. He knew now that he still wanted this girl, and he knew that the past sometimes comes back –

that was all. For the rest he must be strong and watchful and he would see.

'And now,' Mrs Cary was saying, 'I want you two to go and see the lady who has the chrysanthemums. She particularly told me she wanted to see you because she'd read about you in the paper.'

They went to see the lady with the chrysanthemums. They walked along the street, and he recognized with a sort of excitement just how her shorter footsteps always fell in between his own. The lady turned out to be nice, and the chrysanthemums were enormous and extraordinarily beautiful. The lady's gardens were full of them, white and pink and yellow, so that to be among them was a trip back into the heart of summer. There were two gardens full, and a gate between them; when they strolled towards the second garden the lady went first through the gate.

And then a curious thing happened. George stepped aside to let Jonquil pass, but instead of going through she stood still and stared at him for a minute. It was not so much the look, which was not a smile, as it was the moment of silence. They saw each other's eyes, and both took a short, faintly accelerated breath, and then they went on into the second garden. That was all.

The afternoon waned. They thanked the lady and walked home slowly, thoughtfully, side by side. Through dinner, too, they were silent. George told Mr Cary something of what had happened in South America, and managed to let it be known that everything would be plain sailing for him in the future.

Then dinner was over, and he and Jonquil were alone

in the room which had seen the beginning of their love affair and the end. It seemed to him long ago and inexpressibly sad. On the sofa he had felt agony and grief such as he would never feel again. He would never be so weak or so tired and miserable and poor. Yet he knew that that boy of fifteen months before had had something, a trust, a warmth that was gone forever. The sensible thing – they had done the sensible thing. He had traded his youth for strength and carved success out of despair. But with his youth, life had carried away the freshness of his love.

'You won't marry me, will you?' he said quietly.

Jonquil shook her dark head.

'I'm never going to marry,' she answered.

He nodded.

'I'm going on to Washington in the morning,' he said.

'Oh –'

'I have to go. I've got to be in New York by the first, and meanwhile I want to stop off in Washington.'

'Business!'

'No-o,' he said as if reluctantly. 'There's someone there I must see who was very kind to me when I was so – down and out.'

This was invented. There was no one in Washington for him to see – but he was watching Jonquil narrowly, and he was sure that she winced a little, that her eyes closed and then opened wide again.

'But before I go I want to tell you the things that happened to me since I saw you, and, as maybe we won't meet again, I wonder if – if just this once you'd sit in my lap like you used to. I wouldn't ask except since there's no one else – yet – perhaps it doesn't matter.'

She nodded, and in a moment was sitting in his lap as she had sat so often in that vanished spring. The feel of her head against his shoulder, of her familiar body, sent a shock of emotion over him. His arms holding her had a tendency to tighten around her, so he leaned back and began to talk thoughtfully into the air.

He told her of a despairing two weeks in New York which had terminated with an attractive if not very profitable job in a construction plant in Jersey City. When the Peru business had first presented itself it had not seemed an extraordinary opportunity. He was to be third assistant engineer on the expedition, but only ten of the American party, including eight rodmen and surveyors, had ever reached Cuzco. Ten days later the chief of the expedition was dead of yellow fever. That had been his chance, a chance for anybody but a fool, a marvellous chance –

'A chance for anybody but a fool?' she interrupted innocently.

'Even for a fool,' he continued. 'It was wonderful. Well, I wired New York –'

'And so,' she interrupted again, 'they wired that you ought to take a chance?'

'Ought to!' he exclaimed, still leaning back. 'That I *had* to. There was no time to lose –'

'Not a minute?'

'Not a minute.'

'Not even time for –' she paused.

'For what?'

'Look.'

He bent his head forward suddenly, and she drew herself to him in the same moment, her lips half open like a flower.

'Yes,' he whispered into her lips. 'There's all the time in the world . . .'

All the time in the world – his life and hers. But for an instant as he kissed her he knew that though he search through eternity he could never recapture those lost April hours. He might press her close now till the muscles knotted on his arms – she was something desirable and rare that he had fought for and made his own – but never again an intangible whisper in the dusk, or on the breeze of night . . .

Well, let it pass, he thought; April is over, April is over. There are all kinds of love in the world, but never the same love twice.

# The Bridal Party

## I

There was the usual insincere little note saying: 'I wanted you to be the first to know.' It was a double shock to Michael, announcing, as it did, both the engagement and the imminent marriage; which, moreover, was to be held, not in New York, decently and far away, but here in Paris under his very nose, if that could be said to extend over the Protestant Episcopal Church of the Holy Trinity, Avenue Georges-Cinq. The date was two weeks off, early in June.

At first Michael was afraid and his stomach felt hollow. When he left the hotel that morning, the *femme de chambre*, who was in love with his fine, sharp profile and his pleasant buoyancy, scented the hard abstraction that had settled over him. He walked in a daze to his bank, he bought a detective story at Smith's on the Rue de Rivoli, he sympathetically stared for a while at a faded panorama of the battlefields in a tourist-office window and cursed a Greek tout who followed him with a half-displayed packet of innocuous post cards warranted to be very dirty indeed.

But the fear stayed with him, and after a while he recognized it as the fear that now he would never be happy. He had met Caroline Dandy when she was seventeen, possessed her young heart all through her first season in New York, and then lost her, slowly, tragically, uselessly, because he had no money and could make no money; because, with all the energy and good-will in the world, he could not find himself; because, loving him still, Caroline had lost faith and begun to see him as something pathetic, futile, and shabby, outside the great, shining stream of life towards which she was inevitably drawn.

Since his only support was that she loved him, he leaned weakly on that; the support broke, but still he held on to it and was carried out to sea and washed up on the French coast with its broken pieces still in his hands. He carried them around with him in the form of photographs and packets of correspondence and a liking for a maudlin popular song called 'Among My Souvenirs'. He kept clear of other girls, as if Caroline would somehow know it and reciprocate with a faithful heart. Her note informed him that he had lost her forever.

It was a fine morning. In front of the shops in the Rue de Castiglione, proprietors and patrons were on the sidewalk gazing upward, for the Graf Zeppelin, shining and glorious, symbol of escape and destruction – of escape, if necessary, through destruction – glided in the Paris sky. He heard a woman say in French that it would not astonish her if that commenced to let fall the bombs. Then he heard another voice, full of husky laughter, and the void in his stomach froze. Jerking about, he was face to face with Caroline Dandy and her fiancé.

'Why, Michael! Why, we were wondering where you were. I asked at the Guaranty Trust, and Morgan and Company, and finally sent a note to the National City –'

Why didn't they back away? Why didn't they back right up, walking backwards down the Rue de Castiglione, across the Rue de Rivoli, through the Tuileries Gardens, still walking backwards as fast as they could till they grew vague and faded out across the river?

'This is Hamilton Rutherford, my fiancé.'

'We've met before.'

'At Pat's, wasn't it?'

'And last spring in the Ritz Bar.'

'Michael, where have you been keeping yourself?'

'Around here.' This agony. Previews of Hamilton Rutherford flashed before his eyes – a quick series of pictures, sentences. He remembered hearing that he had bought a seat in 1920 for a hundred and twenty-five thousand of borrowed money, and just before the break sold it for more than half a million. Not handsome like Michael, but vitally attractive, confident, authoritative, just the right height over Caroline there – Michael had always been too short for Caroline when they danced.

Rutherford was saying: 'No, I'd like it very much if you'd come to the bachelor dinner. I'm taking the Ritz Bar from nine o'clock on. Then right after the wedding there'll be a reception and breakfast at the Hôtel Georges-Cinq.'

'And, Michael, George Packman is giving a party day after tomorrow at Chez Victor, and I want you to be sure and come. And also to tea Friday at Jebby West's; she'd want to have you if she knew where you were. Where's your hotel, so we can send you an invitation? You see, the reason we decided to have it over here is because mother has been sick in a nursing home here and the whole clan is in Paris. Then Hamilton's mother's being here too –'

The entire clan; they had always hated him, except her mother; always discouraged his courtship. What a little counter he was in this game of families and money! Under his hat his brow sweated with the humiliation of the fact that for all his misery he was worth just exactly so many invitations. Frantically he began to mumble something about going away.

Then it happened – Caroline saw deep into him, and Michael knew that she saw. She saw through to his profound woundedness, and something quivered inside her, died out along the curve of her mouth and in her eyes. He had moved her. All the unforgettable impulses of first love had surged up once more; their hearts had in some way touched across two feet of Paris sunlight. She took her fiancé's arm suddenly, as if to steady herself with the feel of it.

They parted. Michael walked quickly for a minute; then he stopped, pretending to look in a window, and saw them farther up the street, walking fast into the Place Vendôme, people with much to do.

He had things to do also – he had to get his laundry.

'Nothing will ever be the same again,' he said to himself. 'She will never be happy in her marriage and I will never be happy at all any more.'

The two vivid years of his love for Caroline moved back around him like years in Einstein's physics. Intolerable memories arose – of rides in the Long Island moonlight; of a happy time at Lake Placid with her cheeks so cold there, but warm just underneath the surface; of a despairing afternoon in a little café on Forty-eighth Street in the last sad months when their marriage had come to seem impossible.

'Come in,' he said aloud.

The concierge with a telegram; brusque, because Mr Curly's clothes were a little shabby. Mr Curly gave few tips; Mr Curly was obviously a *petit client*.

Michael read the telegram.

'An answer?' the concierge asked.

'No,' said Michael, and then, on an impulse: 'Look.'

'Too bad – too bad,' said the concierge. 'Your grandfather is dead.'

'Not too bad,' said Michael. 'It means that I come into a quarter of a million dollars.'

Too late by a single month; after the first flush of the news his misery was deeper than ever. Lying awake in bed that night, he listened endlessly to the long caravan of a circus moving through the street from one Paris fair to another.

When the last van had rumbled out of hearing and the corners of the furniture were pastel blue with the dawn, he was still thinking of the look in Caroline's eyes that morning – the look that seemed to say: 'Oh, why couldn't you have done something about it? Why couldn't you have been stronger, made me marry you? Don't you see how sad I am?'

Michael's fists clenched.

'Well, I won't give up till the last moment,' he whispered. 'I've had all the bad luck so far, and maybe it's turned at last. One takes what one can get, up to the limit of one's strength, and if I can't have her, at least she'll go into this marriage with some of me in her heart.'

## II

Accordingly he went to the party at Chez Victor two days later, upstairs and into the little salon off the bar where the party was to assemble for cocktails. He was early; the only other occupant was a tall lean man of fifty. They spoke.

'You waiting for George Packman's party?'

'Yes. My name's Michael Curly.'

'My name's –'

Michael failed to catch the name. They ordered a drink, and Michael supposed that the bride and groom were having a gay time.

'Too much so,' the other agreed, frowning. 'I don't see how they stand it. We all crossed on the boat together; five days of that crazy life and then two weeks of Paris. You' – he hesitated, smiling faintly – 'you'll excuse me for saying that your generation drinks too much.'

'Not Caroline.'

'No, not Caroline. She seems to take only a cocktail and a glass of champagne, and then she's had enough, thank God. But Hamilton drinks too much and all this crowd of young people drink too much. Do you live in Paris?'

'For the moment,' said Michael.

'I don't like Paris. My wife – that is to say, my ex-wife, Hamilton's mother – lives in Paris.'

'You're Hamilton Rutherford's father?'

'I have that honour. And I'm not denying that I'm proud of what he's done; it was just a general comment.'

'Of course.'

Michael glanced up nervously as four people came in. He felt suddenly that his dinner coat was old and shiny; he had ordered a new one that morning. The people who had come in were rich and at home in their richness with one another – a dark, lovely girl with a hysterical little laugh whom he had met before; two confident men whose jokes referred invariably to last night's scandal and tonight's potentialities, as if they had important rôles in a play that extended indefinitely into the past and the future. When Caroline arrived, Michael had scarcely a moment of her, but it was enough to note that, like all the others, she was strained and tired. She was pale beneath her rouge; there were shadows under her eyes. With a mixture of relief and wounded vanity, he found himself placed far from her and at another table; he needed a moment to adjust himself to his surroundings. This was not like the immature set in which he and Caroline had moved; the men were more than thirty and had an air of sharing the best of this world's goods. Next to him was Jebby West, whom he knew; and, on the other side, a jovial man who immediately began to talk to Michael about a stunt for the bachelor dinner: They were going to hire a French girl to appear with an actual baby in her arms, crying: 'Hamilton, you can't desert me now!' The idea seemed stale and unamusing to Michael, but its originator shook with anticipatory laughter.

Farther up the table there was talk of the market – another drop today, the most appreciable since the crash; people were kidding Rutherford about it: 'Too bad, old man. You better not get married, after all.'

Michael asked the man on his left, 'Has he lost a lot?'

'Nobody knows. He's heavily involved, but he's one of the smartest young men in Wall Street. Anyhow, nobody ever tells you the truth.'

It was a champagne dinner from the start, and towards the end it reached a pleasant level of conviviality, but Michael saw that all these people were too weary to be exhilarated by any ordinary stimulant; for weeks they had drunk cocktails before meals like Americans, wines and brandies like Frenchmen, beer like Germans, whisky-and-soda like the English, and as they were no longer in the twenties, this preposterous *mélange*, that was like some gigantic cocktail in a nightmare, served only to make them temporarily less conscious of the mistakes of the night before. Which is to say that it was not really a gay party; what gaiety existed was displayed in the few who drank nothing at all.

But Michael was not tired, and the champagne stimulated him and made his misery less acute. He had

been away from New York for more than eight months
and most of the dance music was unfamiliar to him,
but at the first bars of the 'Painted Doll' to which
he and Caroline had moved through so much happiness and despair the previous summer, he crossed to
Caroline's table and asked her to dance.

She was lovely in a dress of thin ethereal blue, and
the proximity of her crackly yellow hair, of her cool
and tender grey eyes, turned his body clumsy and rigid;
he stumbled with their first step on the floor. For a
moment it seemed that there was nothing to say; he
wanted to tell her about his inheritance, but the idea
seemed abrupt, unprepared for.

'Michael, it's so nice to be dancing with you again.'

He smiled grimly.

'I'm so happy you came,' she continued. 'I was afraid
maybe you'd be silly and stay away. Now we can be
just good friends and natural together. Michael, I want
you and Hamilton to like each other.'

The engagement was making her stupid; he had
never heard her make such a series of obvious remarks
before.

'I could kill him without a qualm,' he said pleasantly,
'but he looks like a good man. He's fine. What I want
to know is, what happens to people like me who aren't
able to forget?'

As he said this he could not prevent his mouth from
drooping suddenly, and glancing up, Caroline saw,
and her heart quivered violently, as it had the other
morning.

'Do you mind so much, Michael?'

'Yes.'

For a second as he said this, in a voice that seemed to have come up from his shoes, they were not dancing; they were simply clinging together. Then she leaned away from him and twisted her mouth into a lovely smile.

'I didn't know what to do at first, Michael. I told Hamilton about you – that I'd cared for you an awful lot – but it didn't worry him, and he was right. Because I'm over you now – yes, I am. And you'll wake up some sunny morning and be over me just like that.'

He shook his head stubbornly.

'Oh, yes. We weren't for each other. I'm pretty flighty, and I need somebody like Hamilton to decide things. It was that more than the question of – of –'

'Of money.' Again he was on the point of telling her what had happened, but again something told him it was not the time.

'Then how do you account for what happened when we met the other day,' he demanded helplessly – 'what happened just now? When we just pour towards each other like we used to – as if we were one person, as if the same blood was flowing through both of us?'

'Oh, don't!' she begged him. 'You mustn't talk like that; everything's decided now. I love Hamilton with all my heart. It's just that I remember certain things in the past and I feel sorry for you – for us – for the way we were.'

Over her shoulder, Michael saw a man come towards them to cut in. In a panic he danced her away, but inevitably the man came on.

'I've got to see you alone, if only for a minute,' Michael said quickly. 'When can I?'

'I'll be at Jebby West's tea tomorrow,' she whispered as a hand fell politely upon Michael's shoulder.

But he did not talk to her at Jebby West's tea. Rutherford stood next to her, and each brought the other into all conversations. They left early. The next morning the wedding cards arrived in the first mail.

Then Michael, grown desperate with pacing up and down his room, determined on a bold stroke; he wrote to Hamilton Rutherford, asking him for a rendezvous the following afternoon. In a short telephone communication Rutherford agreed, but for a day later than Michael had asked. And the wedding was only six days away.

They were to meet in the bar of the Hôtel Jéna. Michael knew what he would say: 'See here, Rutherford, do you realize the responsibility you're taking in going through with this marriage? Do you realize the harvest of trouble and regret you're sowing in persuading a girl into something contrary to the instincts of her heart?' He would explain that the barrier between Caroline and himself had been an artificial one and was now removed, and demand that the matter be put up to Caroline frankly before it was too late.

Rutherford would be angry, conceivably there would be a scene, but Michael felt that he was fighting for his life now.

He found Rutherford in conversation with an older man, whom Michael had met at several of the wedding parties.

'I saw what happened to most of my friends,' Rutherford was saying, 'and I decided it wasn't going to happen to me. It isn't so difficult; if you take a girl with common sense, and tell her what's what, and do your stuff damn well, and play decently square with her, it's a marriage. If you stand for any nonsense at the beginning, it's one of these arrangements – within five years the man gets out, or else the girl gobbles him up and you have the usual mess.'

'Right!' agreed his companion enthusiastically. 'Hamilton, boy, you're right.'

Michael's blood boiled slowly.

'Doesn't it strike you,' he inquired coldly, 'that your attitude went out of fashion about a hundred years ago?'

'No, it didn't,' said Rutherford pleasantly, but impatiently. 'I'm as modern as anybody. I'd get married in an aeroplane next Saturday if it'd please my girl.'

'I don't mean that way of being modern. You can't take a sensitive woman –'

'Sensitive? Women aren't so darn sensitive. It's fellows like you who are sensitive; it's fellows like you that they exploit – all your devotion and kindness and all that. They read a couple of books and see a few pictures because they haven't got anything else to do, and then they say they're finer in grain than you are, and to prove it they take the bit in their teeth and tear off for a fare-you-well – just about as sensitive as a fire horse.'

'Caroline happens to be sensitive,' said Michael in a clipped voice.

At this point the other man got up to go; when the dispute about the check had been settled and they were alone, Rutherford leaned back to Michael as if a question had been asked him.

'Caroline's more than sensitive,' he said. 'She's got sense.'

His combative eyes, meeting Michael's, flickered with a grey light. 'This all sounds pretty crude to you, Mr Curly, but it seems to me that the average man nowadays just asks to be made a monkey of by some woman who doesn't even get any fun out of reducing him to that level. There are darn few men who possess their wives any more, but I am going to be one of them.'

To Michael it seemed time to bring the talk back to the actual situation: 'Do you realize the responsibility you're taking?'

'I certainly do,' interrupted Rutherford. 'I'm not afraid of responsibility. I'll make the decisions – fairly, I hope, but anyhow they'll be final.'

'What if you didn't start right?' said Michael impetuously. 'What if your marriage isn't founded on mutual love?'

'I think I see what you mean,' Rutherford said, still pleasant. 'And since you've brought it up, let me say that if you and Caroline had married, it wouldn't have lasted three years. Do you know what your affair was founded on? On sorrow. You got sorry for each other. Sorrow's a lot of fun for most women and for some men, but it seems to me that a marriage ought to be based on hope.' He looked at his watch and stood up.

'I've got to meet Caroline. Remember, you're coming to the bachelor dinner day after tomorrow.'

Michael felt the moment slipping away. 'Then Caroline's personal feelings don't count with you?' he demanded fiercely.

'Caroline's tired and upset. But she has what she wants, and that's the main thing.'

'Are you referring to yourself?' demanded Michael incredulously.

'Yes.'

'May I ask how long she's wanted you?'

'About two years.' Before Michael could answer, he was gone. During the next two days Michael floated in an abyss of helplessness. The idea haunted him that he had left something undone that would sever this knot drawn tight under his eyes. He phoned Caroline, but she insisted that it was physically impossible for her to see him until the day before the wedding, for which day she granted him a tentative rendezvous. Then he went to the bachelor dinner, partly in fear of an evening alone at his hotel, partly from a feeling that by his presence at that function he was somehow nearer to Caroline, keeping her in sight.

The Ritz Bar had been prepared for the occasion by French and American banners and by a great canvas covering one wall, against which the guests were invited to concentrate their proclivities in breaking glasses.

At the first cocktail, taken at the bar, there were many slight spillings from many trembling hands, but later, with the champagne, there was a rising tide of laughter and occasional bursts of song.

Michael was surprised to find what a difference his new dinner coat, his new silk hat, his new, proud linen made in his estimate of himself; he felt less resentment towards all these people for being so rich and assured. For the first time since he had left college he felt rich and assured himself; he felt that he was part of all this, and even entered into the scheme of Johnson, the practical joker, for the appearance of the woman betrayed, now waiting tranquilly in the room across the hall.

'We don't want to go too heavy,' Johnson said, 'because I imagine Ham's had a pretty anxious day already. Did you see Fullman Oil's sixteen points off this morning?'

'Will that matter to him?' Michael asked, trying to keep the interest out of his voice.

'Naturally. He's in heavily; he's always in everything heavily. So far he's had luck: anyhow, up to a month ago.'

The glasses were filled and emptied faster now, and men were shouting at one another across the narrow table. Against the bar a group of ushers was being photographed, and the flash light surged through the room in a stifling cloud.

'Now's the time,' Johnson said. 'You're to stand by the door, remember, and we're both to try and keep her from coming in – just till we get everybody's attention.'

He went on out into the corridor, and Michael waited obediently by the door. Several minutes passed. Then Johnson reappeared with a curious expression on his face.

'There's something funny about this.'

'Isn't the girl there?'

'She's there all right, but there's another woman there, too; and it's nobody we engaged either. She wants to see Hamilton Rutherford, and she looks as if she had something on her mind.'

They went out into the hall. Planted firmly in a chair near the door sat an American girl a little the worse for liquor, but with a determined expression on her face. She looked up at them with a jerk of her head.

'Well, j'tell him?' she demanded. 'The name is Marjorie Collins, and he'll know it. I've come a long way, and I want to see him now and quick, or there's going to be more trouble than you ever saw.' She rose unsteadily to her feet.

'You go in and tell Ham,' whispered Johnson to Michael. 'Maybe he'd better get out. I'll keep her here.'

Back at the table, Michael leaned close to Rutherford's ear and, with a certain grimness, whispered:

'A girl outside named Marjorie Collins says she wants to see you. She looks as if she wanted to make trouble.'

Hamilton Rutherford blinked and his mouth fell ajar; then slowly the lips came together in a straight line and he said in a crisp voice:

'Please keep her there. And send the head barman to me right away.'

Michael spoke to the barman, and then, without returning to the table, asked quietly for his coat and hat. Out in the hall again, he passed Johnson and the girl without speaking and went out into the

Rue Cambon. Calling a cab, he gave the address of Caroline's hotel.

His place was beside her now. Not to bring bad news, but simply to be with her when her house of cards came falling around her head.

Rutherford had implied that he was soft – well, he was hard enough not to give up the girl he loved without taking advantage of every chance within the pale of honour. Should she turn away from Rutherford, she would find him there.

She was in; she was surprised when he called, but she was still dressed and would be down immediately. Presently she appeared in a dinner gown, holding two blue telegrams in her hand. They sat down in armchairs in the deserted lobby.

'But, Michael, is the dinner over?'

'I wanted to see you, so I came away.'

'I'm glad.' Her voice was friendly, but matter-of-fact. 'Because I'd just phoned your hotel that I had fittings and rehearsals all day tomorrow. Now we can have our talk after all.'

'You're tired,' he guessed. 'Perhaps I shouldn't have come.'

'No. I was waiting up for Hamilton. Telegrams that may be important. He said he might go on somewhere, and that may mean any hour, so I'm glad I have someone to talk to.'

Michael winced at the impersonality in the last phrase.

'Don't you care when he gets home?'

'Naturally,' she said, laughing, 'but I haven't got much say about it, have I?'

'Why not?'

'I couldn't start by telling him what he could and couldn't do.'

'Why not?'

'He wouldn't stand for it.'

'He seems to want merely a housekeeper,' said Michael ironically.

'Tell me about your plans, Michael,' she asked quickly.

'My plans? I can't see any future after the day after tomorrow. The only real plan I ever had was to love you.'

Their eyes brushed past each other's, and the look he knew so well was staring out at him from hers. Words flowed quickly from his heart:

'Let me tell you just once more how well I've loved you, never wavering for a moment, never thinking of another girl. And now when I think of all the years ahead without you, without any hope, I don't want to live, Caroline darling. I used to dream about our home, our children, about holding you in my arms and touching your face and hands and hair that used to belong to me, and now I just can't wake up.'

Caroline was crying softly. 'Poor Michael – poor Michael.' Her hand reached out and her fingers brushed the lapel of his dinner coat. 'I was so sorry for you the other night. You looked so thin, and as if you needed a new suit and somebody to take care of you.'

She sniffled and looked more closely at his coat. 'Why, you've got a new suit! And a new silk hat! Why, Michael, how swell!' She laughed, suddenly cheerful through her tears. 'You must have come into money, Michael; I never saw you so well turned out.'

For a moment, at her reaction, he hated his new clothes.

'I have come into money,' he said. 'My grandfather left me about a quarter of a million dollars.'

'Why, Michael,' she cried, 'how perfectly swell! I can't tell you how glad I am. I've always thought you were the sort of person who ought to have money.'

'Yes, just too late to make a difference.'

The revolving door from the street groaned around and Hamilton Rutherford came into the lobby. His face was flushed, his eyes were restless and impatient.

'Hello, darling: hello, Mr Curly.' He bent and kissed Caroline. 'I broke away for a minute to find out if I had any telegrams. I see you've got them there.' Taking them from her, he remarked to Curly, 'That was an odd business there in the bar, wasn't it? Especially as I understand some of you had a joke fixed up in the same line.' He opened one of the telegrams, closed it and turned to Caroline with the divided expression of a man carrying two things in his head at once.

'A girl I haven't seen for two years turned up,' he said. 'It seemed to be some clumsy form of blackmail, for I haven't and never have had any sort of obligation towards her whatever.'

'What happened?'

'The head barman had a Sûreté Générale man there

in ten minutes and it was settled in the hall. The French blackmail laws make ours look like a sweet wish, and I gather they threw a scare into her that she'll remember. But it seems wiser to tell you.'

'Are you implying that I mentioned the matter?' said Michael stiffly.

'No,' Rutherford said slowly. 'No, you were just going to be on hand. And since you're here, I'll tell you some news that will interest you even more.'

He handed Michael one telegram and opened the other.

'This is in code,' Michael said.

'So is this. But I've got to know all the words pretty well this last week. The two of them together mean I'm due to start life all over.'

Michael saw Caroline's face grow a shade paler, but she sat quiet as a mouse.

'It was a mistake and I stuck to it too long,' continued Rutherford. 'So you see I don't have all the luck, Mr Curly. By the way, they tell me you've come into money.'

'Yes,' said Michael.

'There we are, then.' Rutherford turned to Caroline. 'You understand, darling, that I'm not joking or exaggerating. I've lost almost every cent I had and I'm starting life over.'

Two pairs of eyes were regarding her – Rutherford's non-committal and unrequiring, Michael's hungry, tragic, pleading. In a minute she had raised herself from the chair and with a little cry thrown herself into Hamilton Rutherford's arms.

'Oh, darling,' she cried, 'what does it matter! It's better; I like it better, honestly I do! I want to start that way; I want to! Oh, please don't worry or be sad even for a minute!'

'All right, baby,' said Rutherford. His hand stroked her hair gently for a moment; then he took his arm from around her.

'I promised to join the party for an hour,' he said. 'So I'll say good night, and I want you to go to bed soon and get a good sleep. Good night, Mr Curly. I'm sorry to have let you in for all these financial matters.'

But Michael had already picked up his hat and cane. 'I'll go along with you,' he said.


### III


It was such a fine morning. Michael's cutaway hadn't been delivered, so he felt rather uncomfortable passing before the cameras and moving-picture machines in front of the little church on the Avenue Georges-Cinq.

It was such a clean, new church that it seemed unforgivable not to be dressed properly, and Michael, white and shaky after a sleepless night, decided to stand in the rear. From there he looked at the back of Hamilton Rutherford, and the lacy, filmy back of Caroline, and the fat back of George Packman, which looked unsteady, as if it wanted to lean against the bride and groom.

The ceremony went on for a long time under the gay flags and pennons overhead, under the thick beams of June sunlight slanting down through the tall windows upon the well-dressed people.

As the procession, headed by the bride and groom, started down the aisle, Michael realized with alarm he was just where everyone would dispense with the parade stiffness, become informal and speak to him.

So it turned out. Rutherford and Caroline spoke first to him; Rutherford grim with the strain of being married, and Caroline lovelier than he had ever seen her, floating all softly down through the past and forward to the future by the sunlit door.

Michael managed to murmur, 'Beautiful, simply beautiful,' and then other people passed and spoke to him – old Mrs Dandy, straight from her sickbed and looking remarkably well, or carrying it off like the very fine old lady she was; and Rutherford's father and mother, ten years divorced, but walking side by side and looking made for each other and proud. Then all Caroline's sisters and their husbands and her little nephews in Eton suits, and then a long parade, all speaking to Michael because he was still standing paralysed just at that point where the procession broke.

He wondered what would happen now. Cards had been issued for a reception at the Georges-Cinq; an expensive enough place, heaven knew. Would Rutherford try to go through with that on top of those disastrous telegrams? Evidently, for the procession outside was streaming up there through the June morning, three by three and four by four. On the corner the long dresses of girls, five abreast, fluttered many-coloured in the wind. Girls had become gossamer again, perambulatory flora;

such lovely fluttering dresses in the bright noon wind.

Michael needed a drink; he couldn't face that reception line without a drink. Diving into a side doorway of the hotel, he asked for the bar, whither a *chasseur* led him through half a kilometre of new American-looking passages.

But – how did it happen? – the bar was full. There were ten – fifteen men and two – four girls, all from the wedding, all needing a drink. There were cocktails and champagne in the bar; Rutherford's cocktails and champagne, as it turned out, for he had engaged the whole bar and the ballroom and the two great reception rooms and all the stairways leading up and down, and windows looking out over the whole square block of Paris. By and by Michael went and joined the long, slow drift of the receiving line. Through a flowery mist of 'Such a lovely wedding', 'My dear, you were simply lovely', 'You're a lucky man, Rutherford' he passed down the line. When Michael came to Caroline, she took a single step forward and kissed him on the lips, but he felt no contact in the kiss; it was unreal and he floated on away from it. Old Mrs Dandy, who had always liked him, held his hand for a minute and thanked him for the flowers he had sent when he heard she was ill.

'I'm so sorry not to have written; you know, we old ladies are grateful for –' The flowers, the fact that she had not written, the wedding – Michael saw that they all had the same relative importance to her now; she had married off five other children and seen two of the marriages go to pieces, and this scene, so poignant, so confusing to Michael, appeared to her simply a familiar charade in which she had played her part before.

A buffet luncheon with champagne was already being served at small tables and there was an orchestra playing in the empty ballroom. Michael sat down with Jebby West; he was still a little embarrassed at not wearing a morning coat, but he perceived now that he was not alone in the omission and felt better. 'Wasn't Caroline divine?' Jebby West said. 'So entirely self-possessed. I asked her this morning if she wasn't a little nervous at stepping off like this. And she said, "Why should I be? I've been after him for two years, and now I'm just happy, that's all."'

'It must be true,' said Michael gloomily.

'What?'

'What you just said.'

He had been stabbed, but, rather to his distress, he did not feel the wound.

He asked Jebby to dance. Out on the floor, Rutherford's father and mother were dancing together.

'It makes me a little sad, that,' she said. 'Those two hadn't met for years; both of them were married again and she divorced again. She went to the station to meet him when he came over for Caroline's wedding, and invited him to stay at her house in the Avenue du Bois with a whole lot of other people, perfectly proper, but he was afraid his wife would hear about it and not like it, so he went to a hotel. Don't you think that's sort of sad?'

An hour or so later Michael realized suddenly that it was afternoon. In one corner of the ballroom an arrangement of screens like a moving-picture stage had been set up and photographers were taking official pictures of the bridal party. The bridal party, still as death and pale as wax under the bright lights, appeared, to the dancers circling the modulated semi-darkness of the ballroom, like those jovial or sinister groups that one comes upon in The Old Mill at an amusement park.

After the bridal party had been photographed, there was a group of the ushers; then the bridesmaids, the families, the children. Later Caroline, active and excited, having long since abandoned the repose implicit in her flowing dress and great bouquet, came and plucked Michael off the floor.

'Now we'll have them take one of just old friends.' Her voice implied that this was best, most intimate of all. 'Come here, Jebby, George – not you, Hamilton; this is just my friends – Sally –'

A little after that, what remained of formality disappeared and the hours flowed easily down the profuse stream of champagne. In the modern fashion, Hamilton Rutherford sat at the table with his arm about an old girl of his and assured his guests, which included not a few bewildered but enthusiastic Europeans, that the party was not nearly at an end; it was to reassemble at Zelli's after midnight. Michael saw Mrs Dandy, not quite over her illness, rise to go and become caught in polite group after group, and he spoke of it to one of her daughters, who thereupon forcibly abducted her mother and called her car. Michael felt very considerate and proud of himself after having done this, and drank much more champagne.

'It's amazing,' George Packman was telling him
enthusiastically. 'This show will cost Ham about five
thousand dollars, and I understand they'll be just about
his last. But did he countermand a bottle of champagne
or a flower? Not he! He happens to have it – that
young man. Do you know that T. G. Vance offered
him a salary of fifty thousand dollars a year ten minutes
before the wedding this morning? In another year he'll
be back with the millionaires.'

The conversation was interrupted by a plan to carry
Rutherford out on communal shoulders – a plan which
six of them put into effect, and then stood in the
four-o'clock sunshine waving good-bye to the bride
and groom. But there must have been a mistake somewhere, for five minutes later Michael saw both bride
and groom descending the stairway to the reception,
each with a glass of champagne held defiantly on high.

'This is our way of doing things,' he thought. 'Gen-
erous and fresh and free; a sort of Virginia-plantation
hospitality, but at a different pace now, nervous as a
ticker tape.'

Standing unselfconsciously in the middle of the
room to see which was the American ambassador, he
realized with a start that he hadn't really thought of
Caroline for hours. He looked about him with a sort
of alarm, and then he saw her across the room, very
bright and young, and radiantly happy. He saw Rutherford near her, looking at her as if he could never look
long enough, and as Michael watched them they
seemed to recede as he had wished them to do that
day in the Rue de Castiglione – recede and fade off

47

into joys and griefs of their own, into the years that would take the toll of Rutherford's fine pride and Caroline's young, moving beauty; fade far away, so that now he could scarcely see them, as if they were shrouded in something as misty as her white, billowing dress.

Michael was cured. The ceremonial function, with its pomp and its revelry, had stood for a sort of initiation into a life where even his regret could not follow them. All the bitterness melted out of him suddenly and the world reconstituted itself out of the youth and happiness that was all around him, profligate as the spring sunshine. He was trying to remember which one of the bridesmaids he had made a date to dine with tonight as he walked forward to bid Hamilton and Caroline Rutherford good-bye.

# *Magnetism*

## I

The pleasant, ostentatious boulevard was lined at prosperous intervals with New England Colonial houses – without ship models in the hall. When the inhabitants moved out here the ship models had at last been given to the children. The next street was a complete exhibit of the Spanish-bungalow phase of West Coast architecture; while two streets over, the cylindrical windows and round towers of 1897 – melancholy antiques which sheltered swamis, yogis, fortune tellers, dressmakers, dancing teachers, art academies and chiropractors – looked down now upon brisk buses and trolley cars. A little walk around the block could, if you were feeling old that day, be a discouraging affair.

On the green flanks of the modern boulevard children, with their knees marked by the red stains of the mercurochrome era, played with toys with a purpose – beams that taught engineering, soldiers that taught manliness, and dolls that taught motherhood. When the dolls were so banged up that they stopped looking like real babies and began to look like dolls, the children developed affection for them. Everything in the vicinity – even the March sunlight – was new, fresh, hopeful and thin, as you would expect in a city that had tripled its population in fifteen years.

Among the very few domestics in sight that morning was a handsome young maid sweeping the steps of the biggest house on the street. She was a large, simple Mexican girl with the large, simple ambitions of the time and the locality, and she was already conscious of being a luxury – she received one hundred dollars a month in return for her personal liberty. Sweeping. Dolores kept an eye on the stairs inside, for Mr Hannaford's car was waiting and he would soon be coming down to breakfast. The problem came first this morning, however – the problem as to whether it was a duty or a favour when she helped the English nurse down the steps with the perambulator. The English nurse always said 'Please', and 'Thanks very much', but Dolores hated her and would have liked, without any special excitement, to beat her insensible. Like most Latins under the stimulus of American life, she had irresistible impulses towards violence.

The nurse escaped, however. Her blue cape faded haughtily into the distance just as Mr Hannaford, who had come quietly downstairs, stepped into the space of the front door.

'Good morning.' He smiled at Dolores; he was young and extraordinarily handsome. Dolores tripped on the broom and fell off the stoop. George Hannaford hurried down the steps, reached her as she was getting to her feet cursing volubly in Mexican, just touched her arm with a helpful gesture and said, 'I hope you didn't hurt yourself.'

'Oh, no.'

'I'm afraid it was my fault; I'm afraid I startled you, coming out like that.'

His voice had real regret in it; his brow was knit with solicitude,

'Are you sure you're all right?'

'Aw, sure.'

'Didn't turn your ankle?'

'Aw, no.'

'I'm terribly sorry about it.'

'Aw, it wasn't your fault.'

He was still frowning as she went inside, and Dolores, who was not hurt and thought quickly, suddenly contemplated having a love affair with him. She looked at herself several times in the pantry mirror and stood close to him as she poured his coffee, but he read the paper and she saw that that was all for the morning.

Hannaford entered his car and drove to Jules Rennard's house. Jules was a French Canadian by birth, and George Hannaford's best friend; they were fond of each other and spent much time together. Both of them were simple and dignified in their tastes and in their way of thinking, instinctively gentle, and in a world of the volatile and the bizarre found in each other a certain quiet solidity.

He found Jules at breakfast.

'I want to fish for barracuda,' said George abruptly. 'When will you be free? I want to take the boat and go down to Lower California.'

Jules had dark circles under his eyes. Yesterday he had closed out the greatest problem of his life by settling with his ex-wife for two hundred thousand dollars. He had married too young, and the former slavey from the Quebec slums had taken to drugs upon her failure to rise with him. Yesterday, in the presence of lawyers, her final gesture had been to smash his finger with the base of a telephone. He was tired of women for a while and welcomed the suggestion of a fishing trip.

'How's the baby?' he asked.

'The baby's fine.'

'And Kay?'

'Kay's not herself, but I don't pay any attention. What did you do to your hand?'

'I'll tell you another time. What's the matter with Kay, George?'

'Jealous.'

'Of who?'

'Helen Avery. It's nothing. She's not herself, that's all.' He got up. 'I'm late,' he said. 'Let me know as soon as you're free. Any time after Monday will suit me.'

George left and drove out by an interminable boulevard which narrowed into a long, winding concrete road and rose into the hilly country behind. Somewhere in the vast emptiness a group of buildings appeared, a barnlike structure, a row of offices, a large but quick restaurant and half a dozen small bungalows. The chauffeur dropped Hannaford at the main entrance. He went in and passed through various enclosures, each marked off by swinging gates and inhabited by a stenographer.

'Is anybody with Mr Schroeder?' he asked, in front of a door lettered with that name.

'No, Mr Hannaford.'

Simultaneously his eye fell on a young lady who was writing at a desk aside, and he lingered a moment.

'Hello, Margaret,' he said. 'How are you, darling?'

A delicate, pale beauty looked up, frowning a little, still abstracted in her work. It was Miss Donovan, the script girl, a friend of many years.

'Hello. Oh, George, I didn't see you come in. Mr Douglas wants to work on the book sequence this afternoon.'

'All right.'

'These are the changes we decided on Thursday night.' She smiled up at him and George wondered for the thousandth time why she had never gone into pictures.

'All right,' he said. 'Will initials do?'

'Your initials look like George Harris's.'

'Very well, darling.'

As he finished, Pete Schroeder opened his door and beckoned him. 'George, come here!' he said with an air of excitement. 'I want you to listen to some one on the phone.'

Hannaford went in.

'Pick up the phone and say "Hello",' directed Schroeder. 'Don't say who you are.'

'Hello,' said Hannaford obediently.

'Who is this?' asked a girl's voice.

Hannaford put his hand over the mouthpiece. 'What am I supposed to do?'

Schroeder snickered and Hannaford hesitated, smiling and suspicious.

'Who do you want to speak to?' he temporized into the phone.

'To George Hannaford, I want to speak to. Is this him?'

'Yes.'

'Oh, George; it's me.'

'Who?'

'Me – Gwen. I had an awful time finding you. They told me –'

'Gwen who?'

'Gwen – can't you hear? From San Francisco – last Thursday night.'

'I'm sorry,' objected George. 'Must be some mistake.'

'Is this George Hannaford?'

'Yes.'

The voice grew slightly tart: 'Well, this is Gwen Becker you spent last Thursday evening with in San Francisco. There's no use pretending you don't know who I am, because you do.'

Schroeder took the apparatus from George and hung up the receiver.

'Somebody has been doubling for me up in Frisco,' said Hannaford.

'So that's where you were Thursday night!'

'Those things aren't funny to me – not since that crazy Zeller girl. You can never convince them they've been sold because the man always looks something like you. What's new, Pete?'

'Let's go over to the stage and see.'

Together they walked out a back entrance, along a muddy walk, and opening a little door in the big blank wall of the studio building entered into its half darkness.

Here and there figures spotted the dim twilight, figures that turned up white faces to George Hannaford, like souls in purgatory watching the passage of a half-god through. Here and there were whispers and soft voices and, apparently from afar, the gentle tremolo of a small organ. Turning the corner made by some flats, they came upon the white crackling glow of a stage with two people motionless upon it.

An actor in evening clothes, his shirt front, collar and cuffs tinted a brilliant pink, made as though to get chairs for them, but they shook their heads and stood watching. For a long while nothing happened on the stage – no one moved. A row of lights went off with a savage hiss, went on again. The plaintive tap of a hammer begged admission to nowhere in the distance; a blue face appeared among the blinding lights above and called something unintelligible into the upper blackness. Then the silence was broken by a low clear voice from the stage:

'If you want to know why I haven't got stockings on, look in my dressing-room. I spoiled four pairs yesterday and two already this morning . . . This dress weighs six pounds.'

A man stepped out of the group of observers and regarded the girl's brown legs; their lack of covering was scarcely distinguishable, but, in any event, her expression implied that she would do nothing about it.

The lady was annoyed, and so intense was her personality that it had taken only a fractional flexing of her eyes to indicate the fact. She was a dark, pretty girl with a figure that would be full-blown sooner than she wished. She was just eighteen.

Had this been the week before, George Hannaford's heart would have stood still. Their relationship had been in just that stage. He hadn't said a word to Helen Avery that Kay could have objected to, but something had begun between them on the second day of this picture that Kay had felt in the air. Perhaps it had begun even earlier, for he had determined, when he saw Helen Avery's first release, that she should play opposite him. Helen Avery's voice and the dropping of her eyes when she finished speaking, like a sort of exercise in control, fascinated him. He had felt that they both tolerated something, that each knew half of some secret about people and life, and that if they rushed towards each other there would be a romantic communion of almost unbelievable intensity. It was this element of promise and possibility that had haunted him for a fortnight and was now dying away.

Hannaford was thirty, and he was a moving-picture actor only through a series of accidents. After a year in a small technical college he had taken a summer job with an electric company, and his first appearance in a studio was in the role of repairing a bank of Klieg lights. In an emergency he played a small part and made good, but for fully a year after that he thought of it as a purely transitory episode in his life. At first much of it had offended him – the almost hysterical egotism and excitability hidden under an extremely thin veil of elaborate good-fellowship. It was only recently, with the advent of such men as Jules Rennard into pictures, that he began to see the possibilities of a decent and secure private life, much as his would have been as a successful engineer. At last his success felt solid beneath his feet.

He met Kay Tomkins at the old Griffith Studios at Mamaroneck and their marriage was a fresh, personal affair, removed from most stage marriages. Afterwards they had possessed each other completely, had been pointed to: 'Look, there's one couple in pictures who manage to stay together.' It would have taken something out of many people's lives – people who enjoyed a vicarious security in the contemplation of their marriage – if they hadn't stayed together, and their love was fortified by a certain effort to live up to that.

He held women off by a polite simplicity that underneath was hard and watchful; when he felt a certain current being turned on he became emotionally stupid. Kay expected and took much more from men, but she, too, had a careful thermometer against her heart. Until the other night, when she reproached him for being interested in Helen Avery, there had been an absolute minimum of jealousy between them.

George Hannaford was still absorbed in the thought of Helen Avery as he left the studio and walked towards his bungalow over the way. There was in his mind, first, a horror that anyone should come between him and Kay, and second, a regret that he no longer carried that possibility in the forefront of his mind. It had given him a tremendous pleasure, like the things that had happened to him during his first big success, before he was so 'made' that there was scarcely anything better ahead; it was something to take out and look at – a new and still mysterious joy. It hadn't been love, for he was critical of Helen Avery as he had never been critical of Kay. But his feeling of last week had been sharply significant and memorable, and he was restless, now that it had passed.

Working that afternoon, they were seldom together, but he was conscious of her and he knew that she was conscious of him.

She stood a long time with her back to him at one point, and when she turned at length, their eyes swept past each other's, brushing like bird wings. Simultaneously he saw they had gone far, in their way; it was well that he had drawn back. He was glad that someone came for her when the work was almost over.

Dressed, he returned to the office wing, stopping in for a moment to see Schroeder. No one answered his knock, and, turning the knob, he went in. Helen Avery was there alone.

Hannaford shut the door and they stared at each other. Her face was young, frightened. In a moment in which neither of them spoke, it was decided that they would have some of this out now. Almost thankfully he felt the warm sap of emotion flow out of his heart and course through his body.

'Helen!'

She murmured 'What?' in an awed voice.

'I feel terribly about this.' His voice was shaking.

Suddenly she began to cry; painful, audible sobs shook her. 'Have you got a handkerchief?' she said.

He gave her a handkerchief. At that moment there were steps outside. George opened the door halfway just in time to keep Schroeder from entering on the spectacle of her tears.

'Nobody's in,' he said facetiously. For a moment longer he kept his shoulder against the door. Then he let it open slowly.

Outside in his limousine, he wondered how soon Jules would be ready to go fishing.

## II

From the age of twelve Kay Tompkins had worn men like rings on every finger. Her face was round, young, pretty and strong; a strength accentuated by the responsive play of brows and lashes around her clear, glossy, hazel eyes. She was the daughter of a senator from a Western state and she hunted unsuccessfully for glamour through a small Western city until she was seventeen, when she ran away from home and went on the stage. She was one of those people who are famous far beyond their actual achievement.

There was that excitement about her that seemed to reflect the excitement of the world. While she was playing small parts in Ziegfeld shows she attended proms at Yale, and during a temporary venture into pictures she met George Hannaford, already a star of the new 'natural' type then just coming into vogue. In him she found what she had been seeking.

She was at present in what is known as a dangerous state. For six months she had been helpless and dependent entirely upon George, and now that her son was the property of a strict and possessive English nurse, Kay, free again, suddenly felt the need of proving herself attractive. She wanted things to be as they had been before the baby was thought of. Also she felt that lately George had taken her too much for granted; she had a strong instinct that he was interested in Helen Avery.

When George Hannaford came home that night he had minimized to himself their quarrel of the previous evening and was honestly surprised at her perfunctory greeting.

'What's the matter, Kay?' he asked after a minute. 'Is this going to be another night like last night?'

'Do you know we're going out tonight?' she said, avoiding an answer.

'Where?'

'To Katherine Davis'. I didn't know whether you'd want to go –'

'I'd like to go.'

'I didn't know whether you'd want to go. Arthur Busch said he'd stop for me.'

They dined in silence. Without any secret thoughts to dip into like a child into a jam jar, George felt restless, and at the same time was aware that the atmosphere was full of jealousy, suspicion and anger. Until recently they had preserved between them something precious that made their house one of the pleasantest in Hollywood to enter. Now suddenly it might be any house; he felt common and he felt unstable. He had come near to making something bright and precious into something cheap and unkind. With a sudden surge of emotion, he crossed the room and was about to put his arm around her when the doorbell rang. A moment later Dolores announced Mr Arthur Busch.

Busch was an ugly, popular little man, a continuity writer and lately a director. A few years ago they had been hero and heroine to him, and even now, when he was a person of some consequence in the picture world, he accepted with equanimity Kay's use of him for such purposes as tonight's. He had been in love with her for years, but, because his love seemed hopeless, it had never caused him much distress.

They went on to the party. It was a housewarming, with Hawaiian musicians in attendance, and the guests were largely of the old crowd. People who had been in the early Griffith pictures, even though they were scarcely thirty, were considered to be of the old crowd; they were different from those coming along now, and they were conscious of it. They had a dignity and straightforwardness about them from the fact that they had worked in pictures before pictures were bathed in a golden haze of success. They were still rather humble before their amazing triumph, and thus, unlike the new generation, who took it all for granted, they were constantly in touch with reality. Half a dozen or so of the women were especially aware of being unique. No one had come along to fill their places; here and there a pretty face had caught the public imagination for a year, but those of the old crowd were already legends, ageless and disembodied. With all this, they were still young enough to believe that they would go forever.

George and Kay were greeted affectionately; people moved over and made place for them. The Hawaiians performed and the Ducan sisters sang at the piano. From the moment George saw who was here he guessed that Helen Avery would be here, too, and the fact annoyed him. It was not appropriate that she should be part of this gathering through which he and Kay had moved familiarly and tranquilly for years.

He saw her first when someone opened the swinging door to the kitchen, and when, a little later, she came out and their eyes met, he knew absolutely that he didn't love her. He went up to speak to her, and at her first words he saw something had happened to her, too, that had dissipated the mood of the afternoon. She had got a big part.

'And I'm in a daze!' she cried happily. 'I didn't think there was a chance and I've thought of nothing else since I read the book a year ago.'

'It's wonderful. I'm awfully glad.'

He had the feeling, though, that he should look at her with a certain regret; one couldn't jump from such a scene as this afternoon to a plane of casual friendly interest. Suddenly she began to laugh.

'Oh, we're such actors, George – you and I.'

'What do you mean?'

'You know what I mean.'

'I don't.'

'Oh, yes, you do. You did this afternoon. It was a pity we didn't have a camera.'

Short of declaring then and there that he loved her, there was absolutely nothing more to say. He grinned acquiescently. A group formed around them and absorbed them, and George, feeling that the evening had settled something, began to think about going home. An excited and sentimental elderly lady – someone's mother – came up and began telling him how much she believed in him, and he was polite and charming to her, as only he could be, for half an hour. Then he went to Kay, who had been sitting with Arthur Busch all evening, and suggested that they go.

She looked up unwillingly. She had had several high-balls and the fact was mildly apparent. She did not want to go, but she got up after a mild argument and George went upstairs for his coat. When he came down Katherine Davis told him that Kay had already gone out to the car.

The crowd had increased; to avoid a general good-night he went out through the sun-parlour door to the lawn; less than twenty feet away from him he saw the figures of Kay and Arthur Busch against a bright street lamp; they were standing close together and staring into each other's eyes. He saw that they were holding hands.

After the first start of surprise George instinctively turned about, retraced his steps, hurried through the room he had just left, and came noisily out the front door. But Kay and Arthur Busch were still standing close together, and it was lingeringly and with abstracted eyes that they turned around finally and saw him. Then both of them seemed to make an effort; they drew apart as if it was a physical ordeal. George said good-bye to Arthur Busch with special cordiality, and in a moment he and Kay were driving homeward through the clear California night.

He said nothing, Kay said nothing. He was incredulous. He suspected that Kay had kissed a man here and there, but he had never seen it happen or given it any thought. This was different; there had been an element of tenderness in it and there was something veiled and remote in Kay's eyes that he had never seen there before.

Without having spoken, they entered the house; Kay stopped by the library door and looked in.

'There's someone there,' she said, and she added without interest: 'I'm going upstairs. Good night.'

As she ran up the stairs the person in the library stepped out into the hall.

'Mr Hannaford –'

He was a pale and hard young man; his face was vaguely familiar, but George didn't remember where he had seen it before.

'Mr Hannaford?' said the young man. 'I recognize you from your pictures.' He looked at George, obviously a little awed.

'What can I do for you?'

'Well, will you come in here?'

'What is it? I don't know who you are.'

'My name is Donovan. I'm Margaret Donovan's brother.' His face toughened a little.

'Is anything the matter?'

Donovan made a motion towards the door. 'Come in here.' His voice was confident now, almost threatening.

George hesitated, then he walked into the library. Donovan followed and stood across the table from him, his legs apart, his hands in his pockets.

'Hannaford,' he said, in the tone of a man trying to whip himself up to anger. 'Margaret wants fifty thousand dollars.'

'What the devil are you talking about?' exclaimed George incredulously.

'Margaret wants fifty thousand dollars,' repeated Donovan.

'You're Margaret Donovan's brother?'

'I am.'

'I don't believe it.' But he saw the resemblance now. 'Does Margaret know you're here?'

'She sent me here. She'll hand over those two letters for fifty thousand, and no questions asked.'

'What letters?' George chuckled irresistibly. 'This is some joke of Schroeder's, isn't it?'

'This ain't a joke, Hannaford. I mean the letters you signed your name to this afternoon.'

## III

An hour later George went upstairs in a daze. The clumsiness of the affair was at once outrageous and astounding. That a friend of seven years should suddenly request his signature on papers that were not what they were purported to be made all his surroundings seem diaphanous and insecure. Even now the design engrossed him more than a defence against it, and he tried to re-create the steps by which Margaret had arrived at this act of recklessness or despair.

She had served as a script girl in various studios and for various directors for ten years; earning first twenty, now a hundred dollars a week. She was lovely-looking and she was intelligent; at any moment in those years she might have asked for a screen test, but some quality of initiative or ambition had been lacking. Not a few times had her opinion made or broken incipient careers. Still she waited at directors' elbows, increasingly aware that the years were slipping away.

That she had picked George as a victim amazed him most of all. Once, during the year before his marriage, there had been a momentary warmth; he had taken her to a Mayfair ball, and he remembered that he had kissed her going home that night in the car. The flirtation trailed along hesitatingly for a week. Before it could develop into anything serious he had gone East and met Kay.

Young Donovan had shown him a carbon of the letters he had signed. They were written on the typewriter that he kept in his bungalow at the studio, and they were carefully and convincingly worded. They purported to be love letters, asserting that he was Margaret Donovan's lover, that he wanted to marry her, and that for that reason he was about to arrange a divorce. It was incredible. Someone must have seen him sign them that morning; someone must have heard her say: 'Your initials are like Mr Harris's.'

George was tired. He was training for a screen football game to be played next week, with the Southern California varsity as extras, and he was used to regular hours. In the middle of a confused and despairing sequence of thought about Margaret Donovan and Kay, he suddenly yawned. Mechanically he went upstairs, undressed and got into bed.

Just before dawn Kay came to him in the garden. There was a river that flowed past it now, and boats faintly lit with green and yellow lights moved slowly, remotely by. A gentle starlight fell like rain upon the dark, sleeping face of the world, upon the black mysterious bosoms of the trees, the tranquil gleaming water and the farther shore.

The grass was damp, and Kay came to him on hurried feet; her thin slippers were drenched with dew. She stood upon his shoes, nestling close to him, and held up her face as one shows a book open at a page.

'Think how you love me,' she whispered. 'I don't ask you to love me always like this, but I ask you to remember.'

'You'll always be like this to me.'

'Oh no; but promise me you'll remember.' Her tears were falling. 'I'll be different, but somewhere lost inside me there'll always be the person I am tonight.'

The scene dissolved slowly but George struggled into consciousness. He sat up in bed; it was morning. In the yard outside he heard the nurse instructing his son in the niceties of behaviour for two-month-old babies. From the yard next door a small boy shouted mysteriously: 'Who let that barrier through on me?'

Still in his pyjamas, George went to the phone and called his lawyers. Then he rang for his man, and while he was being shaved a certain order evolved from the chaos of the night before. First, he must deal with Margaret Donovan; second, he must keep the matter from Kay, who in her present state might believe anything; and third, he must fix things up with Kay. The last seemed the most important of all.

As he finished dressing he heard the phone ring downstairs and, with an instinct of danger, picked up the receiver.

'Hello . . . Oh, yes.' Looking up, he saw that both his doors were closed. 'Good morning, Helen . . . It's all right, Dolores. I'm taking it up here.' He waited till he heard the receiver click downstairs.

'How are you this morning, Helen?'

'George, I called up about last night. I can't tell you how sorry I am.'

'Sorry? Why are you sorry?'

'For treating you like that. I don't know what was in me, George. I didn't sleep all night thinking how terrible I'd been.'

A new disorder established itself in George's already littered mind.

'Don't be silly,' he said. To his despair he heard his own voice run on: 'For a minute I didn't understand, Helen. Then I thought it was better so.'

'Oh, George,' came her voice after a moment, very low.

Another silence. He began to put in a cuff button.

'I had to call up,' she said after a moment. 'I couldn't leave things like that.'

The cuff button dropped to the floor; he stooped to pick it up, and then said 'Helen!' urgently into the mouthpiece to cover the fact that he had momentarily been away.

'What, George?'

At this moment the hall door opened and Kay, radiating a faint distaste, came into the room. She hesitated.

'Are you busy?'

'It's all right.' He stared into the mouthpiece for a moment.

'Well, good-bye,' he muttered abruptly and hung up the receiver. He turned to Kay: 'Good morning.'

'I didn't mean to disturb you,' she said distantly.

'You didn't disturb me.' He hesitated. 'That was Helen Avery.'

'It doesn't concern me who it was. I came to ask you if we're going to the Coconut Grove tonight.'

'Sit down, Kay.'

'I don't want to talk.'

'Sit down a minute,' he said impatiently. She sat down. 'How long are you going to keep this up?' he demanded.

'I'm not keeping up anything. We're simply through, George, and you know it as well as I do.'

'That's absurd,' he said. 'Why, a week ago –'

'It doesn't matter. We've been getting nearer to this for months, and now it's over.'

'You mean you don't love me?' He was not particularly alarmed. They had been through scenes like this before.

'I don't know. I suppose I'll always love you in a way.' Suddenly she began to sob. 'Oh, it's all so sad. He's cared for me so long.'

George stared at her. Face to face with what was apparently a real emotion, he had no words of any kind. She was not angry, not threatening or pretending, not thinking about him at all, but concerned entirely with her emotions towards another man.

'What is it?' he cried. 'Are you trying to tell me you're in love with this man?'

'I don't know,' she said helplessly.

He took a step towards her, then went to the bed and lay down on it, staring in misery at the ceiling. After a while a maid knocked to say that Mr Busch and Mr Castle, George's lawyer, were below. The fact carried no meaning to him. Kay went into her room and he got up and followed her.

'Let's send word we're out,' he said. 'We can go away somewhere and talk this over.'

'I don't want to go away.'

She was already away, growing more mysterious and remote with every minute. The things on her dressing-table were the property of a stranger.

He began to speak in a dry, hurried voice. 'If you're still thinking about Helen Avery, it's nonsense. I've never given a damn for anybody but you.'

They went downstairs and into the living-room. It was nearly noon – another bright emotionless California day. George saw that Arthur Busch's ugly face in the sunshine was wan and white; he took a step towards George and then stopped, as if he were waiting for something – a challenge, a reproach, a blow.

In a flash the scene that would presently take place ran itself off in George's mind. He saw himself moving through the scene, saw his part, an infinite choice of parts, but in every one of them Kay would be against him and with Arthur Busch. And suddenly he rejected them all.

'I hope you'll excuse me,' he said quickly to Mr Castle. 'I called you up because a script girl named Margaret Donovan wants fifty thousand dollars for some letters she claims I wrote her. Of course the whole thing is –' He broke off. It didn't matter. 'I'll come to see you tomorrow.' He walked up to Kay and Arthur, so that only they could hear.

'I don't know about you two – what you want to do. But leave me out of it; you haven't any right to inflict any of it on me, for after all it's not my fault. I'm not going to be mixed up in your emotions.'

He turned and went out. His car was before the door and he said 'Go to Santa Monica' because it was the first name that popped into his head. The car drove off into the everlasting hazeless sunlight.

He rode for three hours, past Santa Monica and then along towards Long Beach by another road. As if it were something he saw out of the corner of his eye and with but a fragment of his attention, he imagined

Kay and Arthur Busch progressing through the afternoon. Kay would cry a great deal and the situation would seem harsh and unexpected to them at first, but the tender closing of the day would draw them together. They would turn inevitably towards each other and he would slip more and more into the position of the enemy outside.

Kay had wanted him to get down in the dirt and dust of a scene and scramble for her. Not he; he hated scenes. Once he stooped to compete with Arthur Busch in pulling at Kay's heart, he would never be the same to himself. He would always be a little like Arthur Busch; they would always have that in common, like a shameful secret. There was little of the theatre about George; the millions before whose eyes the moods and changes of his face had flickered during ten years had not been deceived about that. From the moment when, as a boy of twenty, his handsome eyes had gazed off into the imaginary distance of a Griffith Western, his audience had been really watching the progress of a straightforward, slow-thinking, romantic man through an accidentally glamorous life.

His fault was that he had felt safe too soon. He realized suddenly that the two Fairbankses, in sitting side by side at table, were not keeping up a pose. They were giving hostages to fate. This was perhaps the most bizarre community in the rich, wild, bored empire, and for a marriage to succeed here, you must expect nothing or you must be always together. For a moment his glance had wavered from Kay and he stumbled blindly into disaster.

As he was thinking this and wondering where he would go and what he should do, he passed an apartment house that jolted his memory. It was on the outskirts of town, a pink horror built to represent something, somewhere, so cheaply and sketchily that whatever it copied the architect must have long since forgotten. And suddenly George remembered that he had once called for Margaret Donovan here the night of a Mayfair dance.

'Stop at this apartment!' he called through the speaking-tube.

He went in. The negro elevator boy stared open-mouthed at him as they rose in the cage. Margaret Donovan herself opened the door.

When she saw him she shrank away with a little cry. As he entered and closed the door she retreated before him into the front room. George followed.

It was twilight outside and the apartment was dusky and sad. The last light fell softly on the standardized furniture and the great gallery of signed photographs of moving-picture people that covered one wall. Her face was white, and as she stared at him she began nervously wringing her hands.

'What's this nonsense, Margaret?' George said, try-ing to keep any reproach out of his voice. 'Do you need money that bad?'

She shook her head vaguely. Her eyes were still fixed on him with a sort of terror; George looked at the floor.

'I suppose this was your brother's idea. At least I can't believe you'd be so stupid.' He looked up, trying to preserve the brusque masterly attitude of one talking to a naughty child, but at the sight of her face every emotion except pity left him. 'I'm a little tired. Do you mind if I sit down?'

'No.'

'I'm a little confused today,' said George after a minute. 'People seem to have it in for me today.'

'Why, I thought' – her voice became ironic in mid-sentence – 'I thought everybody loved you, George.'

'They don't.'

'Only me?'

'Yes,' he said abstractedly.

'I wish it had been only me. But then, of course, you wouldn't have been you.'

Suddenly he realized that she meant what she was saying.

'That's just nonsense.'

'At least you're here,' Margaret went on. 'I suppose I ought to be glad of that. And I am. I most decidedly am. I've often thought of you sitting in that chair, just at this time when it was almost dark. I used to make up little one-act plays about what would happen then. Would you like to hear one of them? I'll have to begin by coming over and sitting on the floor at your feet.'

Annoyed and yet spellbound, George kept trying desperately to seize upon a word or mood that would turn the subject.

'I've seen you sitting there so often that you don't look a bit more real than your ghost. Except that your hat has squashed your beautiful hair down on one side and you've got dark circles or dirt under your eyes. You look white, too, George. Probably you were on a party last night.'

'I was. And I found your brother waiting for me when I got home.'

'He's a good waiter, George. He's just out of San Quentin prison, where he's been waiting the last six years.'

'Then it was his idea?'

'We cooked it up together. I was going to China on my share.'

'Why was I the victim?'

'That seemed to make it realer. Once I thought you were going to fall in love with me five years ago.'

The bravado suddenly melted out of her voice and it was still light enough to see that her mouth was quivering.

'I've loved you for years,' she said – 'since the first day you came West and walked into the old Realart Studio. You were so brave about people, George. Whoever it was, you walked right up to them and tore something aside as if it was in your way and began to know them. I tried to make love to you, just like the rest, but it was difficult. You drew people right up close to you and held them there, not able to move either way.'

'This is all entirely imaginary,' said George, frowning uncomfortably, 'and I can't control –'

'No, I know. You can't control charm. It's simply got to be used. You've got to keep your hand in if you have it, and go through life attaching people to you that you don't want. I don't blame you. If you only hadn't kissed me the night of the Mayfair dance. I suppose it was the champagne.'

George felt as if a band which had been playing for a long time in the distance had suddenly moved up and taken a station beneath his window. He had always been conscious that things like this were going on around him. Now that he thought of it, he had always been conscious that Margaret loved him, but the faint music of these emotions in his ear had seemed to bear no relation to actual life. They were phantoms that he had conjured up out of nothing; he had never imagined their actual incarnations. At his wish they should die inconsequently away.

'You can't imagine what it's been like,' Margaret continued after a minute. 'Things you've just said and forgotten, I've put myself asleep night after night remembering – trying to squeeze something more out of them. After that night you took me to the Mayfair other men didn't exist for me any more. And there were others, you know – lots of them. But I'd see you walking along somewhere about the lot, looking at the ground and smiling a little, as if something very amusing had just happened to you, the way you do. And I'd pass you and you'd look up and really smile: "Hello, darling!" "Hello, darling" and my heart would turn over. That would happen four times a day.'

George stood up and she, too, jumped up quickly.

'Oh, I've bored you,' she cried softly. 'I might have known I'd bore you. You want to go home. Let's see –

is there anything else? Oh, yes; you might as well have those letters.'

Taking them out of a desk, she took them to a window and identified them by a rift of lamplight.

'They're really beautiful letters. They'd do you credit. I suppose it was pretty stupid, as you say, but it ought to teach you a lesson about – about signing things, or something.' She tore the letters small and threw them in the wastebasket: 'Now go on,' she said.

'Why must I go now?'

For the third time in twenty-four hours sad and uncontrollable tears confronted him.

'Please go!' she cried angrily – 'or stay if you like. I'm yours for the asking. You know it. You can have any woman you want in the world by just raising your hand. Would I amuse you?'

'Margaret –'

'Oh, go on then.' She sat down and turned her face away. 'After all you'll begin to look silly in a minute. You wouldn't like that, would you? So get out.'

George stood there helpless, trying to put himself in her place and say something that wouldn't be priggish, but nothing came.

He tried to force down his personal distress, his discomfort, his vague feeling of scorn, ignorant of the fact that she was watching him and understanding it all and loving the struggle in his face. Suddenly his own nerves gave way under the strain of the past twenty-four hours and he felt his eyes grow dim and his throat tighten. He shook his head helplessly. Then he turned away – still not knowing that she was watching him and loving him until she thought her heart would burst with it – and went out to the door.

## IV

The car stopped before his house, dark save for small lights in the nursery and the lower hall. He heard the telephone ringing, but when he answered it, inside, there was no one on the line. For a few minutes he wandered about in the darkness, moving from chair to chair and going to the window to stare out into the opposite emptiness of the night.

It was strange to be alone, to feel alone. In his over-wrought condition the fact was not unpleasant. As the trouble of last night had made Helen Avery infinitely remote, so his talk with Margaret had acted as a cathar-sis to his own personal misery. It would swing back upon him presently, he knew, but for a moment his mind was too tired to remember, to imagine or to care.

Half an hour passed. He saw Dolores issue from the kitchen, take the paper from the front steps and carry it back to the kitchen for a preliminary inspection. With a vague idea of packing his grip, he went upstairs. He opened the door of Kay's room and found her lying down.

For a moment he didn't speak, but moved around the bathroom between. Then he went into her room and switched on the lights.

'What's the matter?' he asked casually. 'Aren't you feeling well?'

'I've been trying to get some sleep,' she said. 'George, do you think that girl's gone crazy?'

'What girl?'

'Margaret Donovan. I've never heard of anything so terrible in my life.'

For a moment he thought that there had been some new development.

'Fifty thousand dollars!' she cried indignantly. 'Why, I wouldn't give it to her even if it were true. She ought to be sent to jail.'

'Oh, it's not so terrible as that,' he said. 'She has a brother who's a pretty bad egg and it was his idea.'

'She's capable of anything,' Kay said solemnly. 'And you're just a fool if you don't see it. I've never liked her. She has dirty hair.'

'Well, what of it?' he demanded impatiently, and added: 'Where's Arthur Busch?'

'He went home right after lunch. Or rather I sent him home.'

'You decided you were not in love with him?'

She looked up almost in surprise. 'In love with him? Oh, you mean this morning. I was just mad at you; you ought to have known that. I was a little sorry for him last night, but I guess it was the highballs.'

'Well, what did you mean when you –' He broke off. Wherever he turned he found a muddle, and he resolutely determined not to think.

'My heavens!' exclaimed Kay. 'Fifty thousand dollars!'

'Oh, drop it. She tore up the letters – she wrote them herself – and everything's all right.'

'George.'

'Yes.'

'Of course Douglas will fire her right away.'

'Of course he won't. He won't know anything about it.'

'You mean to say you're not going to let her go? After this?'

He jumped up. 'Do you suppose she thought that?' he cried.

'Thought what?'

'That I'd have them let her go?'

'You certainly ought to.'

He looked hastily through the phone book for her name.

'Oxford –' he called.

After an unusually long time the switchboard operator answered: 'Bourbon Apartments.'

'Miss Margaret Donovan, please.'

'Why –' The operator's voice broke off. 'If you'll just wait a minute, please.' He held the line; the minute passed, then another. Then the operator's voice: 'I couldn't talk to you then. Miss Donovan has had an accident. She's shot herself. When you called they were taking her through the lobby to St Catherine's Hospital.'

'Is she – is it serious?' George demanded frantically.

'They thought so at first, but now they think she'll be all right. They're going to probe for the bullet.'

'Thank you.'

He got up and turned to Kay.

'She's tried to kill herself,' he said in a strained voice.

'I'll have to go around to the hospital. I was pretty clumsy this afternoon and I think I'm partly responsible for this.'

'George,' said Kay suddenly.

'What?'

'Don't you think it's sort of unwise to get mixed up in this? People might say –'

'I don't give a damn what they say,' he answered roughly.

He went to his room and automatically began to prepare for going out. Catching sight of his face in the mirror, he closed his eyes with a sudden exclamation of distaste, and abandoned the intention of brushing his hair.

'George,' Kay called from the next room, 'I love you.'

'I love you too.'

'Jules Rennard called up. Something about barracuda fishing. Don't you think it would be fun to get up a party? Men and girls both?'

'Somehow the idea doesn't appeal to me. The whole idea of barracuda fishing –'

The phone rang below and he started. Dolores was answering it.

It was a lady who had already called twice today.

'Is Mr Hannaford in?'

'No,' said Dolores promptly. She stuck out her tongue and hung up the phone just as George Hanna-ford came downstairs. She helped him into his coat, standing as close as she could to him, opened the door and followed a little way out on the porch.

'Meester Hannaford,' she said suddenly, 'that Miss Avery she call up five-six times today. I tell her you out and say nothing to missus.'

'What?' He stared at her, wondering how much she knew about his affairs.

'She call up just now and I say you out.'

'All right,' he said absently.

'Meester Hannaford.'

'Yes, Dolores.'

'I deedn't hurt myself thees morning when I fell off the porch.'

'That's fine. Good night, Dolores.'

'Good night, Meester Hannaford.'

George smiled at her, faintly, fleetingly, tearing a veil from between them, unconsciously promising her a possible admission to the thousand delights and wonders that only he knew and could command. Then he went to his waiting car and Dolores, sitting down on the stoop, rubbed her hands together in a gesture that might have expressed either ecstasy or strangulation, and watched the rising of the thin, pale California moon.

# Bernice Bobs Her Hair

## I

After dark on Saturday night one could stand on the first tee of the golf-course and see the country-club windows as a yellow expanse over a very black and wavy ocean. The waves of this ocean, so to speak, were the heads of many curious caddies, a few of the more ingenious chauffeurs, the golf professional's deaf sister – and there were usually several stray, diffident waves who might have rolled inside had they so desired. This was the gallery.

The balcony was inside. It consisted of the circle of wicker chairs that lined the wall of the combination club-room and ballroom. At these Saturday-night dances it was largely feminine; a great babel of middle-aged ladies with sharp eyes and icy hearts behind lorgnettes and large bosoms. The main function of the balcony was critical. It occasionally showed grudging admiration, but never approval, for it is well known among ladies over thirty-five that when the younger set dance in the summer-time it is with the very worst intentions in the world, and if they are not bombarded with stony eyes stray couples will dance weird barbaric interludes in the corners, and the more popular, more

83

dangerous, girls will sometimes be kissed in the parked limousines of unsuspecting dowagers.

But, after all, this critical circle is not close enough to the stage to see the actors' faces and catch the subtler byplay. It can only frown and lean, ask questions and make satisfactory deductions from its set of postulates, such as the one which states that every young man with a large income leads the life of a hunted partridge. It never really appreciates the drama of the shifting, semi-cruel world of adolescence. No; boxes, orchestra-circle, principals, and chorus are represented by the medley of faces and voices that sway to the plaintive African rhythm of Dyer's dance orchestra.

From sixteen-year-old Otis Ormonde, who has two more years at Hill School, to G. Reece Stoddard, over whose bureau at home hangs a Harvard law diploma; from little Madeleine Hogue, whose hair still feels strange and uncomfortable on top of her head, to Bessie MacRae, who has been the life of the party a little too long – more than ten years – the medley is not only the centre of the stage but contains the only people capable of getting an unobstructed view of it.

With a flourish and a bang the music stops. The couples exchange artificial, effortless smiles, facetiously repeat '*la*-de-*da-da* dum-*dum*,' and then the clatter of young feminine voices soars over the burst of clapping.

A few disappointed stags caught in midfloor as they had been about to cut in subsided listlessly back to the walls, because this was not like the riotous Christmas dances – these summer hops were considered just pleasantly warm and exciting, where even the younger marrieds rose and performed ancient waltzes and terrifying fox trots to the tolerant amusement of their younger brothers and sisters.

Warren McIntyre, who casually attended Yale, being one of the unfortunate stags, felt in his dinner-coat pocket for a cigarette and strolled out onto the wide, semi-dark veranda, where couples were scattered at tables, filling the lantern-hung night with vague words and hazy laughter. He nodded here and there at the less absorbed and as he passed each couple some half-forgotten fragment of a story played in his mind, for it was not a large city and everyone was Who's Who to every one else's past. There, for example, were Jim Strain and Ethel Demorest, who had been privately engaged for three years. Everyone knew that as soon as Jim managed to hold a job for more than two months she would marry him. Yet how bored they both looked, and how wearily Ethel regarded Jim sometimes, as if she wondered why she had trained the vines of her affection on such a wind-shaken poplar.

Warren was nineteen and rather pitying with those of his friends who hadn't gone East to college. But, like most boys, he bragged tremendously about the girls of his city when he was away from it. There was Genevieve Ormonde, who regularly made the rounds of dances, house-parties, and football games at Princeton, Yale, Williams, and Cornell; there was black-eyed Roberta Dillon, who was quite as famous to her own generation as Hiram Johnson or Ty Cobb; and, of course, there was Marjorie Harvey, who besides having a fairylike face and a dazzling, bewildering tongue was already justly celebrated for having turned five cartwheels in succession during the past pump-and-slipper dance at New Haven.

Warren, who had grown up across the street from Marjorie, had long been 'crazy about her'. Sometimes she seemed to reciprocate his feeling with a faint gratitude, but she had tried him by her infallible test and informed him gravely that she did not love him. Her test was that when she was away from him she forgot him and had affairs with other boys. Warren found this discouraging, especially as Marjorie had been making little trips all summer, and for the first two or three days after each arrival home he saw great heaps of mail on the Harveys' hall table addressed to her in various masculine handwritings. To make matters worse, all during the month of August she had been visited by her cousin Bernice from Eau Claire, and it seemed impossible to see her alone. It was always necessary to hunt round and find some one to take care of Bernice. As August waned this was becoming more and more difficult.

Much as Warren worshipped Marjorie, he had to admit that Cousin Bernice was sorta dopeless. She was pretty, with dark hair and high colour, but she was no fun on a party. Every Saturday night he danced a long arduous duty dance with her to please Marjorie, but he had never been anything but bored in her company.

'Warren' – a soft voice at his elbow broke in upon his thoughts, and he turned to see Marjorie, flushed and radiant as usual. She laid a hand on his shoulder and a glow settled almost imperceptibly over him.

'Warren,' she whispered, 'do something for me – dance with Bernice. She's been stuck with little Otis Ormonde for almost an hour.'

Warren's glow faded.

'Why – sure,' he answered half-heartedly.

'You don't mind, do you? I'll see that you don't get stuck.'

''Sall right.'

Marjorie smiled – that smile that was thanks enough.

'You're an angel, and I'm obliged loads.'

With a sigh the angel glanced round the veranda, but Bernice and Otis were not in sight. He wandered back inside, and there in front of the women's dressing-room he found Otis in the centre of a group of young men who were convulsed with laughter. Otis was brandishing a piece of timber he had picked up, and discoursing volubly.

'She's gone in to fix her hair,' he announced wildly. 'I'm waiting to dance another hour with her.'

Their laughter was renewed.

'Why don't some of you cut in?' cried Otis resentfully. 'She likes more variety.'

'Why, Otis,' suggested a friend, 'you've just barely got used to her.'

'Why the two-by-four, Otis?' inquired Warren, smiling.

'The two-by-four? Oh, this? This is a club. When she comes out I'll hit her on the head and knock her in again.'

Warren collapsed on a settee and howled with glee.

'Never mind, Otis,' he articulated finally. 'I'm relieving you this time.'

Otis simulated a sudden fainting attack and handed the stick to Warren.

'If you need it, old man,' he said hoarsely.

No matter how beautiful or brilliant a girl may be, the reputation of not being frequently cut in on makes her position at a dance unfortunate. Perhaps boys prefer her company to that of the butterflies with whom they dance a dozen times an evening, but youth in this jazz-nourished generation is temperamentally restless, and the idea of fox-trotting more than one full fox trot with the same girl is distasteful, not to say odious. When it comes to several dances and the intermissions between she can be quite sure that a young man, once relieved, will never tread on her wayward toes again.

Warren danced the next full dance with Bernice, and finally, thankful for the intermission, he led her to a table on the veranda. There was a moment's silence while she did unimpressive things with her fan.

'It's hotter here than in Eau Claire,' she said.

Warren stifled a sigh and nodded. It might be for all he knew or cared. He wondered idly whether she was a poor conversationalist because she got no attention or got no attention because she was a poor conversationalist.

'You going to be here much longer?' he asked, and then turned rather red. She might suspect his reasons for asking.

'Another week,' she answered, and stared at him as if to lunge at his next remark when it left his lips.

Warren fidgeted. Then with a sudden charitable impulse he decided to try part of his line on her. He turned and looked at her eyes.

'You've got an awfully kissable mouth,' he began quietly.

This was a remark that he sometimes made to girls at college proms when they were talking in just such half dark as this. Bernice distinctly jumped. She turned an ungraceful red and became clumsy with her fan. No one had ever made such a remark to her before.

'Fresh!' – the word had slipped out before she realized it, and she bit her lip. Too late she decided to be amused, and offered him a flustered smile.

Warren was annoyed. Though not accustomed to have that remark taken seriously, still it usually provoked a laugh or a paragraph of sentimental banter. And he hated to be called fresh, except in a joking way. His charitable impulse died and he switched the topic.

'Jim Strain and Ethel Demorest sitting out as usual,' he commented.

This was more in Bernice's line, but a faint regret mingled with her relief as the subject changed. Men did not talk to her about kissable mouths, but she knew that they talked in some such way to other girls.

'Oh, yes,' she said, and laughed. 'I hear they've been mooning round for years without a red penny. Isn't it silly?'

Warren's disgust increased. Jim Strain was a close friend of his brother's, and anyway he considered it bad form to sneer at people for not having money. But

Bernice had had no intention of sneering. She was merely nervous.

## II

When Marjorie and Bernice reached home at half after midnight they said good night at the top of the stairs. Though cousins, they were not intimates. As a matter of fact Marjorie had no female intimates – she considered girls stupid. Bernice on the contrary all through this parent-arranged visit had rather longed to exchange those confidences flavoured with giggles and tears that she considered an indispensable factor in all feminine intercourse. But in this respect she found Marjorie rather cold; felt somehow the same difficulty in talking to her that she had in talking to men. Marjorie never giggled, was never frightened, seldom embarrassed, and in fact had very few of the qualities which Bernice considered appropriately and blessedly feminine.

As Bernice busied herself with tooth-brush and paste this night she wondered for the hundredth time why she never had any attention when she was away from home. That her family were the wealthiest in Eau Claire; that her mother entertained tremendously, gave little dinners for her daughter before all dances and bought her a car of her own to drive round in, never occurred to her as factors in her home-town social success. Like most girls she had been brought up on the warm milk prepared by Annie Fellows Johnston and on novels in which the female was beloved because of certain mysterious womanly qualities, always mentioned but never displayed.

Bernice felt a vague pain that she was not at present engaged in being popular. She did not know that had it not been for Marjorie's campaigning she would have danced the entire evening with one man; but she knew that even in Eau Claire other girls with less position and less pulchritude were given a much bigger rush. She attributed this to something subtly unscrupulous in those girls. It had never worried her, and if it had her mother would have assured her that the other girls cheapened themselves and that men really respected girls like Bernice.

She turned out the light in her bathroom, and on an impulse decided to go in and chat for a moment with her aunt Josephine whose light was still on. Her soft slippers bore her noiselessly down the carpeted hall, but hearing voices inside she stopped near the partly opened door. Then she caught her own name, and without any definite intention of eavesdropping lingered – and the thread of the conversation going on inside pierced her consciousness sharply as if it had been drawn through with a needle.

'She's absolutely hopeless!' It was Marjorie's voice. 'Oh, I know what you're going to say! So many people have told you how pretty and sweet she is, and how she can cook! What of it? She has a bum time. Men don't like her.'

'What's a little cheap popularity?'

Mrs Harvey sounded annoyed.

'It's everything when you're eighteen,' said Marjorie emphatically. 'I've done my best. I've been polite and I've made men dance with her, but they just won't stand being bored. When I think of that gorgeous colouring wasted on such a ninny, and think what Martha Carey could do with it – oh!'

'There's no courtesy these days.'

Mrs Harvey's voice implied that modern situations were too much for her. When she was a girl all young ladies who belonged to nice families had glorious times.

'Well,' said Marjorie, 'no girl can permanently bolster up a lame-duck visitor, because these days it's every girl for herself. I've even tried to drop her hints about clothes and things, and she's been furious – given me the funniest looks. She's sensitive enough to know she's not getting away with much, but I'll bet she consoles herself by thinking that she's very virtuous and that I'm too gay and fickle and will come to a bad end. All unpopular girls think that way. Sour grapes! Sarah Hopkins refers to Genevieve and Roberta and me as gardenia girls! I'll bet she'd give ten years of her life and her European education to be a gardenia girl and have three or four men in love with her and be cut in on every few feet at dances.'

'It seems to me,' interrupted Mrs Harvey rather wearily, 'that you ought to be able to do something for Bernice. I know she's not very vivacious.'

Marjorie groaned.

'Vivacious! Good grief! I've never heard her say anything to a boy except that it's hot or the floor's crowded or that she's going to school in New York next year.

Sometimes she asks them what kind of car they have and tells them the kind she has. Thrilling!'

There was a short silence, and then Mrs Harvey took up her refrain:

'All I know is that other girls not half so sweet and attractive get partners. Martha Carey, for instance, is stout and loud, and her mother is distinctly common. Roberta Dillon is so thin this year that she looks as though Arizona were the place for her. She's dancing herself to death.'

'But, mother,' objected Marjorie impatiently, 'Martha is cheerful and awfully witty and an awfully slick girl, and Roberta's a marvellous dancer. She's been popular for ages!'

Mrs Harvey yawned.

'I think it's that crazy Indian blood in Bernice,' continued Marjorie. 'Maybe she's a reversion to type. Indian women all just sat round and never said anything.'

'Go to bed, you silly child,' laughed Mrs Harvey. 'I wouldn't have told you that if I'd thought you were going to remember it. And I think most of your ideas are perfectly idiotic,' she finished sleepily.

There was another silence, while Marjorie considered whether or not convincing her mother was worth the trouble. People over forty can seldom be permanently convinced of anything. At eighteen our convictions are hills from which we look; at forty-five they are caves in which we hide.

Having decided this, Marjorie said good night. When she came out into the hall it was quite empty.

## III

While Marjorie was breakfasting late next day Bernice came into the room with a rather formal good morning, sat down opposite, stared intently over and slightly moistened her lips.

'What's on your mind?' inquired Marjorie, rather puzzled.

Bernice paused before she threw her hand-grenade.

'I heard what you said about me to your mother last night.'

Marjorie was startled, but she showed only a faintly heightened colour and her voice was quite even when she spoke.

'Where were you?'

'In the hall. I didn't mean to listen – at first.'

After an involuntary look of contempt Marjorie dropped her eyes and became very interested in balancing a stray corn-flake on her finger.

'I guess I'd better go back to Eau Claire – if I'm such a nuisance.' Bernice's lower lip was trembling violently and she continued on a wavering note: 'I've tried to be nice, and – and I've been first neglected and then insulted. No one ever visited me and got such treatment.'

Marjorie was silent.

'But I'm in the way, I see. I'm a drag on you. Your friends don't like me.' She paused, and then remembered another one of her grievances. 'Of course I was furious last week when you tried to hint to me that

that dress was unbecoming. Don't you think I know how to dress myself?'

'No,' murmured Marjorie less than half-aloud.

'What?'

'I didn't hint anything,' said Marjorie succinctly. 'I said, as I remember, that it was better to wear a becoming dress three times straight than to alternate it with two frights.'

'Do you think that was a very nice thing to say?'

'I wasn't trying to be nice.' Then after a pause: 'When do you want to go?'

Bernice drew in her breath sharply.

'Oh!' It was a little half-cry.

Marjorie looked up in surprise.

'Didn't you say you were going?'

'Yes, but –'

'Oh, you were only bluffing!'

They stared at each other across the breakfast-table for a moment. Misty waves were passing before Bernice's eyes, while Marjorie's face wore that rather hard expression that she used when slightly intoxicated undergraduates were making love to her.

'So you were bluffing,' she repeated as if it were what she might have expected.

Bernice admitted it by bursting into tears. Marjorie's eyes showed boredom.

'You're my cousin,' sobbed Bernice. 'I'm v-v-visiting you. I was to stay a month, and if I go home my mother will know and she'll wah-wonder –'

Marjorie waited until the shower of broken words collapsed into little sniffles.

'I'll give you my month's allowance,' she said coldly, and 'you can spend this last week anywhere you want. There's a very nice hotel –'

Bernice's sobs rose to a flute note, and rising of a sudden she fled from the room.

An hour later, while Marjorie was in the library absorbed in composing one of those non-committal, marvellously elusive letters that only a young girl can write, Bernice reappeared, very red-eyed and consciously calm. She cast no glance at Marjorie but took a book at random from the shelf and sat down as if to read. Marjorie seemed absorbed in her letter and continued writing. When the clock showed noon Bernice closed her book with a snap.

'I suppose I'd better get my railroad ticket.'

This was not the beginning of the speech she had rehearsed upstairs, but as Marjorie was not getting her cues – wasn't urging her to be reasonable; it's all a mistake – it was the best opening she could muster.

'Just wait till I finish this letter,' said Marjorie without looking round. 'I want to get it off in the next mail.'

After another minute, during which her pen scratched busily, she turned round and relaxed with an air of 'at your service'. Again Bernice had to speak.

'Do you want me to go home?'

'Well,' said Marjorie, considering, 'I suppose if you're not having a good time you'd better go. No use being miserable.'

'Don't you think common kindness –'

'Oh, please don't quote "Little Women"!' cried Marjorie impatiently. 'That's out of style.'

'You think so?'

'Heavens, yes! What modern girl could live like those inane females?'

'They were the models for our mothers.'

Marjorie laughed.

'Yes, they were – not! Besides, our mothers were all very well in their way, but they know very little about their daughters' problems.'

Bernice drew herself up.

'Please don't talk about my mother.'

Marjorie laughed,

'I don't think I mentioned her.'

Bernice felt that she was being led away from her subject.

'Do you think you've treated me very well?'

'I've done my best. You're rather hard material to work with.'

The lids of Bernice's eyes reddened.

'I think you're hard and selfish, and you haven't a feminine quality in you.'

'Oh, my Lord!' cried Marjorie in desperation. 'You little nut! Girls like you are responsible for all the tiresome colourless marriages; all those ghastly inefficiencies that pass as feminine qualities. What a blow it must be when a man with imagination marries the beautiful bundle of clothes that he's been building ideals round, and finds that she's just a weak, whining, cowardly mass of affectations!'

Bernice's mouth had slipped half open.

'The womanly woman!' continued Marjorie. 'Her whole early life is occupied in whining criticisms of girls like me who really do have a good time.'

Bernice's jaw descended farther as Marjorie's voice rose.

'There's some excuse for an ugly girl whining. If I'd been irretrievably ugly I'd never have forgiven my parents for bringing me into the world. But you're starting life without any handicap –' Majorie's little fist clinched. 'If you expect me to weep with you you'll be disappointed. Go or stay, just as you like.' And picking up her letters she left the room.

Bernice claimed a headache and failed to appear at luncheon. They had a matinée date for the afternoon, but the headache persisting, Marjorie made explanations to a not very downcast boy. But when she returned late in the afternoon she found Bernice with a strangely set face waiting for her in her bedroom.

'I've decided,' began Bernice without preliminaries, 'that maybe you're right about things – possibly not. But if you'll tell me why your friends aren't – aren't interested in me, I'll see if I can do what you want me to.'

Marjorie was at the mirror shaking down her hair.

'Do you mean it?'

'Yes.'

'Without reservations? Will you do exactly what I say?'

'Well, I –'

'Well nothing! Will you do exactly as I say?'

'If they're sensible things.'

'They're not! You're no case for sensible things.'

'Are you going to make – to recommend –'

'Yes, everything. If I tell you to take boxing lessons you'll have to do it. Write home and tell your mother you're going to stay another two weeks.'

'If you'll tell me –'

'All right – I'll just give you a few examples now. First, you have no ease of manner. Why? Because you're never sure about your personal appearance. When a girl feels that she's perfectly groomed and dressed she can forget that part of her. That's charm. The more parts of yourself you can afford to forget the more charm you have.'

'Don't I look all right?'

'No; for instance, you never take care of your eyebrows. They're black and lustrous, but by leaving them straggly they're a blemish. They'd be beautiful if you'd take care of them in one-tenth of the time you take doing nothing. You're going to brush them so that they'll grow straight.'

Bernice raised the brows in question.

'Do you mean to say that men notice eyebrows?'

'Yes – subconsciously. And when you go home you ought to have your teeth straightened a little. It's almost imperceptible, still –'

'But I thought,' interrupted Bernice in bewilderment, 'that you despised little dainty feminine things like that.'

'I hate dainty minds,' answered Marjorie. 'But a girl has to be dainty in person. If she looks like a million dollars she can talk about Russia, ping-pong, or the League of Nations and get away with it.'

'What else?'

'Oh, I'm just beginning! There's your dancing.'

'Don't I dance all right?'

'No, you don't – you lean on a man; yes, you do – ever so slightly. I noticed it when we were dancing together yesterday. And you dance standing up straight instead of bending over a little. Probably some old lady on the sideline once told you that you looked so dignified that way. But except with a very small girl it's much harder on the man, and he's the one that counts.'

'Go on,' Bernice's brain was reeling.

'Well, you've got to learn to be nice to men who are sad birds. You look as if you'd been insulted whenever you're thrown with any except the most popular boys. Why, Bernice, I'm cut in on every few feet – and who does most of it? Why, those very sad birds. No girl can afford to neglect them. They're the big part of any crowd. Young boys too shy to talk are the very best conversational practice. Clumsy boys are the best dancing practice. If you can follow them and yet look graceful you can follow a baby tank across a barb-wire skyscraper.'

Bernice sighed profoundly, but Marjorie was not through.

'If you go to a dance and really amuse, say, three sad birds that dance with you; if you talk so well to them that they forget they're stuck with you, you've done something. They'll come back next time, and gradually so many sad birds will dance with you that the attractive boys will see there's no danger of being stuck – then they'll dance with you.'

'Yes,' agreed Bernice faintly. 'I think I begin to see.'

'And finally,' concluded Marjorie, 'poise and charm will just come. You'll wake up some morning knowing you've attained it, and men will know it too.'

Bernice rose.

'It's been awfully kind of you – but nobody's ever talked to me like this before, and I feel sort of startled.'

Marjorie made no answer but gazed pensively at her own image in the mirror.

'You're a peach to help me,' continued Bernice.

Still Marjorie did not answer, and Bernice thought she had seemed too grateful.

'I know you don't like sentiment,' she said timidly.

Marjorie turned to her quickly.

'Oh, I wasn't thinking about that. I was considering whether we hadn't better bob your hair.'

Bernice collapsed backward upon the bed.

## IV

On the following Wednesday evening there was a dinner-dance at the country club. When the guests strolled in Bernice found her place-card with a slight feeling of irritation. Though at her right sat G. Reece Stoddard, a most desirable and distinguished young bachelor, the all-important left held only Charley Paulson. Charley lacked height, beauty, and social shrewdness, and in her new enlightenment Bernice decided that his only qualification to be her partner was that he had never been stuck with her. But this feeling of irritation left with the last of the soup-plates, and Marjorie's specific instruction came to her. Swallowing her pride she turned to Charley Paulson and plunged.

'Do you think I ought to bob my hair, Mr Charley Paulson?'

Charley looked up in surprise.

'Why?'

'Because I'm considering it. It's such a sure and easy way of attracting attention.'

Charley smiled pleasantly. He could not know this had been rehearsed. He replied that he didn't know much about bobbed hair. But Bernice was there to tell him.

'I want to be a society vampire, you see,' she announced coolly, and went on to inform him that bobbed hair was the necessary prelude. She added that she wanted to ask his advice, because she had heard he was so critical about girls.

Charley, who knew as much about the psychology of women as he did of the mental states of Buddhist contemplatives, felt vaguely flattered.

'So I've decided,' she continued, her voice rising slightly, 'that early next week I'm going down to the Sevier Hotel barber-shop, sit in the first chair, and get my hair bobbed.' She faltered, noticing that the people near her had paused in their conversation and were listening; but after a confused second Marjorie's coaching told, and she finished her paragraph to the vicinity at large. 'Of course I'm charging admission, but if you'll all come down and encourage me I'll issue passes for the inside seats.'

There was a ripple of appreciative laughter, and under cover of it G. Reece Stoddard leaned over quickly and said to her ear: 'I'll take a box right now.'

She met his eyes and smiled as if he had said something surpassingly brilliant.

'Do you believe in bobbed hair?' asked G. Reece in the same undertone.

'I think it's unmoral,' affirmed Bernice gravely. 'But, of course, you've either got to amuse people or feed 'em or shock 'em.' Marjorie had culled this from Oscar Wilde. It was greeted with a ripple of laughter from the men and a series of quick, intent looks from the girls. And then as though she had said nothing of wit or moment Bernice turned again to Charley and spoke confidentially in his ear.

'I want to ask you your opinion of several people. I imagine you're a wonderful judge of character.'

Charley thrilled faintly – paid her a subtle compliment by overturning her water.

Two hours later, while Warren McIntyre was standing passively in the stag line abstractedly watching the dancers and wondering whither and with whom Marjorie had disappeared, an unrelated perception began to creep slowly upon him – a perception that Bernice, cousin to Marjorie, had been cut in on several times in the past five minutes. He closed his eyes, opened them and looked again. Several minutes back she had been dancing with a visiting boy, a matter easily accounted for; a visiting boy would know no better. But now she was dancing with some one else, and there was Charley Paulson headed for her with enthusiastic determination in his eye. Funny – Charley seldom danced with more than three girls an evening.

Warren was distinctly surprised when – the exchange having been effected – the man relieved proved to be none other than G. Reece Stoddard himself. And G. Reece seemed not at all jubilant at being relieved. Next time Bernice danced near, Warren regarded her intently. Yes, she was pretty, distinctly pretty; and tonight her face seemed really vivacious. She had that look that no woman, however histrionically proficient, can successfully counterfeit – she looked as if she were having a good time. He liked the way she had her hair arranged, wondering if it was brilliantine that made it glisten so. And that dress was becoming – a dark red that set off her shadowy eyes and high colouring. He remembered that he had thought her pretty when she first came to town, before he had realized that she was dull. Too bad she was dull – dull girls were unbearable – certainly pretty though.

His thoughts zigzagged back to Marjorie. This disappearance would be like other disappearances. When she reappeared he would demand where she had been – would be told emphatically that it was none of his business. What a pity she was so sure of him! She basked in the knowledge that no other girl in town interested him; she defied him to fall in love with Genevieve or Roberta.

Warren sighed. The way to Marjorie's affections was a labyrinth indeed. He looked up. Bernice was again dancing with the visiting boy. Half unconsciously he took a step out from the stag line in her direction, and hesitated. Then he said to himself that it was charity. He walked towards her – collided suddenly with G. Reece Stoddard.

'Pardon me,' said Warren.

But G. Reece had not stopped to apologize. He had again cut in on Bernice.

That night at one o'clock Marjorie, with one hand on the electric-light switch in the hall, turned to take a last look at Bernice's sparkling eyes.

'So it worked?'

'Oh, Marjorie, yes!' cried Bernice.

'I saw you were having a gay time.'

'I did! The only trouble was that about midnight I ran short of talk. I had to repeat myself – with different men of course. I hope they won't compare notes.'

'Men don't,' said Marjorie, yawning, 'and it wouldn't matter if they did – they'd think you were even trickier.'

She snapped out the light, and as they started up the stairs Bernice grasped the banister thankfully. For the first time in her life she had been danced tired.

'You see,' said Marjorie at the top of the stairs, 'one man sees another man cut in and he thinks there must be something there. Well, we'll fix up some new stuff tomorrow. Good night.'

'Good night.'

As Bernice took down her hair she passed the evening before her in review. She had followed instructions exactly. Even when Charley Paulson cut in for the eighth time she had simulated delight and had apparently been both interested and flattered. She had not talked about the weather or Eau Claire or automobiles or her school, but had confined her conversation to me, you, and us.

But a few minutes before she fell asleep a rebellious thought was churning drowsily in her brain – after all, it was she who had done it. Marjorie, to be sure, had given her her conversation, but then Marjorie got much of her conversation out of things she read. Bernice had bought the red dress, though she had never valued it highly before Marjorie dug it out of her trunk – and her own voice had said the words, her own lips had smiled, her own feet had danced. Marjorie nice girl – vain, though – nice evening – nice boys – like Warren – Warren – Warren – what's-his-name – Warren –

She fell asleep.

## V

To Bernice the next week was a revelation. With the feeling that people really enjoyed looking at her and listening to her came the foundation of self-confidence. Of course there were numerous mistakes at first. She did not know, for instance, that Draycott Deyo was studying for the ministry; she was unaware that he had cut in on her because he thought she was a quiet, reserved girl. Had she known these things she would not have treated him to the line which began 'Hello, Shell Shock!' and continued with the bathtub story –

'It takes a frightful lot of energy to fix my hair in the summer – there's so much of it – so I always fix it first and powder my face and put on my hat; then I get into the bathtub, and dress afterwards. Don't you think that's the best plan?'

Though Draycott Deyo was in the throes of difficulties concerning baptism by immersion and might possibly have seen a connexion, it must be admitted that he did not. He considered feminine bathing an immoral subject, and gave her some of his ideas on the depravity of modern society.

But to offset that unfortunate occurrence Bernice had several signal successes to her credit. Little Otis Ormonde pleaded off from a trip East and elected instead to follow her with a puppy-like devotion, to the amusement of his crowd and to the irritation of G. Reece Stoddard, several of whose afternoon calls Otis completely ruined by the disgusting tenderness of the glances he bent on Bernice. He even told her the story of the two-by-four and the dressing-room to show her how frightfully mistaken he and everyone else had been in their first judgement of her. Bernice laughed off that incident with a slight sinking sensation.

Of all Bernice's conversation perhaps the best known and most universally approved was the line about the bobbing of her hair.

'Oh, Bernice, when you goin' to get the hair bobbed?'

'Day after tomorrow maybe,' she would reply, laughing. 'Will you come and see me? Because I'm counting on you, you know.'

'Will we? You know! But you better hurry up.'

Bernice, whose tonsorial intentions were strictly dishonourable, would laugh again.

'Pretty soon now. You'd be surprised.'

But perhaps the most significant symbol of her success was the grey car of the hypercritical Warren McIntyre, parked daily in front of the Harvey house. At first the parlourmaid was distinctly startled when he asked for Bernice instead of Marjorie; after a week of it she told the cook that Miss Bernice had gotta hold Miss Marjorie's best fella.

And Miss Bernice had. Perhaps it began with Warren's desire to rouse jealousy in Marjorie; perhaps it was the familiar though unrecognized strain of Marjorie in Bernice's conversation; perhaps it was both of these and something of sincere attraction besides. But somehow the collective mind of the younger set knew within a week that Marjorie's most reliable beau had made an amazing face-about and was giving an indisputable rush to Marjorie's guest. The question of the moment was how Marjorie would take it. Warren called Bernice on the phone twice a day, sent her notes, and they were frequently seen together in his roadster, obviously engrossed in one of those tense, significant conversations as to whether or not he was sincere.

Marjorie on being twitted only laughed. She said she was mighty glad that Warren had at last found someone who appreciated him. So the younger set laughed, too, and guessed that Marjorie didn't care and let it go at that.

One afternoon when there were only three days left of her visit Bernice was waiting in the hall for Warren, with whom she was going to a bridge party. She was in rather a blissful mood, and when Marjorie – also bound for the party – appeared beside her and began casually to adjust her hat in the mirror, Bernice was utterly unprepared for anything in the nature of a clash. Marjorie did her work very coldly and succinctly in three sentences.

'You may as well get Warren out of your head,' she said coldly.

'What?' Bernice was utterly astounded.

'You may as well stop making a fool of yourself over Warren McIntyre. He doesn't care a snap of his fingers about you.'

For a tense moment they regarded each other – Marjorie scornful, aloof; Bernice astounded, half-angry, half-afraid. Then two cars drove up in front of the house and there was a riotous honking. Both of them gasped faintly, turned, and side by side hurried out.

All through the bridge party Bernice strove in vain to master a rising uneasiness. She had offended Marjorie, the sphinx of sphinxes, With the most wholesome and innocent intentions in the world she had stolen Marjorie's property. She felt suddenly and horribly guilty. After the bridge game, when they sat in an informal circle and the conversation became general, the storm gradually broke. Little Otis Ormonde inadvertently precipitated it.

'When you going back to kindergarten, Otis?' some one had asked.

'Me? Day Bernice gets her hair bobbed.'

'Then your education's over,' said Marjorie quickly.

'That's only a bluff of hers. I should think you'd have realized.'

'That a fact?' demanded Otis, giving Bernice a reproachful glance.

Bernice's ears burned as she tried to think up an effectual comeback. In the face of this direct attack her imagination was paralysed.

'There's a lot of bluffs in the world,' continued Marjorie quite pleasantly. 'I should think you'd be young enough to know that, Otis.'

'Well,' said Otis, 'maybe so. But gee! With a line like Bernice's –'

'Really?' yawned Marjorie. 'What's her latest bon mot?'

No one seemed to know. In fact, Bernice, having trifled with her muse's beau, had said nothing memorable of late.

'Was that really all a line?' asked Roberta curiously.

Bernice hesitated. She felt that wit in some form was demanded of her, but under her cousin's suddenly frigid eyes she was completely incapacitated.

'I don't know,' she stalled.

'Splush!' said Marjorie. 'Admit it!'

Bernice saw that Warren's eyes had left a ukulele he had been tinkering with and were fixed on her questioningly.

'Oh, I don't know!' she repeated steadily. Her cheeks were glowing.

'Splush!' remarked Marjorie again.

'Come through, Bernice,' urged Otis. 'Tell her where to get off.'

Bernice looked round again – she seemed unable to get away from Warren's eyes.

'I like bobbed hair,' she said hurriedly, as if he had asked her a question, 'and I intend to bob mine.'

'When?' demanded Marjorie.

'Any time.'

'No time like the present,' suggested Roberta.

Otis jumped to his feet.

'Good stuff!' he cried. 'We'll have a summer bobbing party. Sevier Hotel barber-shop, I think you said.'

In an instant all were on their feet. Bernice's heart throbbed violently.

'What?' she gasped.

Out of the group came Marjorie's voice, very clear and contemptuous.

'Don't worry – she'll back out!'

'Come on, Bernice!' cried Otis, starting towards the door.

Four eyes – Warren's and Marjorie's – stared at her, challenged her, defied her. For another second she wavered wildly.

'All right,' she said swiftly, 'I don't care if I do.'

An eternity of minutes later, riding down-town through the late afternoon beside Warren, the others following in Roberta's car close behind, Bernice had all the sensations of Marie Antoinette bound for the guillotine in a tumbrel. Vaguely she wondered why she did not cry out that it was all a mistake. It was all she could do to keep from clutching her hair with both hands to protect it from the suddenly hostile world. Yet she did neither. Even the thought of her mother was no deterrent now. This was the test supreme of her sportsmanship; her right to walk unchallenged in the starry heaven of popular girls.

Warren was moodily silent, and when they came to the hotel he drew up at the kerb and nodded to Bernice to precede him out. Roberta's car emptied a laughing crowd into the shop, which presented two bold plate-glass windows to the street.

Bernice stood on the kerb and looked at the sign, Sevier Barber-Shop. It was a guillotine indeed, and the hangman was the first barber, who, attired in a white coat and smoking a cigarette, leaned nonchalantly against the first chair. He must have heard of her; he must have been waiting all week, smoking eternal cigarettes beside that portentous, too-often-mentioned first chair. Would they blindfold her? No, but they would tie a white cloth round her neck lest any of her blood – nonsense – hair – should get on her clothes.

'All right, Bernice,' said Warren quickly.

With her chin in the air she crossed the sidewalk, pushed open the swinging screen-door, and giving not a glance to the uproarious, riotous row that occupied the waiting bench, went up to the first barber.

'I want you to bob my hair.'

The first barber's mouth slid somewhat open. His cigarette dropped to the floor.

'Huh?'

'My hair – bob it!'

Refusing further preliminaries, Bernice took her seat on high. A man in the chair next to her turned on his side and gave her a glance, half lather, half amazement.

One barber started and spoiled little Willy Schune-man's monthly haircut. Mr O'Reilly in the last chair grunted and swore musically in ancient Gaelic as a razor bit into his cheek. Two bootblacks became wide-eyed and rushed for her feet. No, Bernice didn't care for a shine.

Outside a passer-by stopped and stared; a couple joined him; half a dozen small boys' noses sprang into life, flattened against the glass; and snatches of conversation borne on the summer breeze drifted in through the screen-door.

'Lookada long hair on a kid!'

'Where'd yuh get 'at stuff? 'At's a bearded lady he just finished shavin'.'

But Bernice saw nothing, heard nothing. Her only living sense told her that this man in the white coat had removed one tortoiseshell comb and then another; that his fingers were fumbling clumsily with unfamiliar hairpins; that this hair, this wonderful hair of hers, was going – she would never again feel its long voluptuous pull as it hung in a dark-brown glory down her back. For a second she was near breaking down, and then the picture before her swam mechanically into her vision – Marjorie's mouth curling in a faint ironic smile as if to say:

'Give up and get down! You tried to buck me and I called your bluff. You see you haven't got a prayer.'

And some last energy rose up in Bernice, for she clenched her hands under the white cloth, and there was a curious narrowing of her eyes that Marjorie remarked on to someone long afterward.

Twenty minutes later the barber swung her round to face the mirror, and she flinched at the full extent of the damage that had been wrought. Her hair was not curly, and now it lay in lank lifeless blocks on both sides of her suddenly pale face. It was ugly as sin – she had known it would be ugly as sin. Her face's chief charm had been a Madonna-like simplicity. Now that was gone and she was – well, frightfully mediocre – not stagy; only ridiculous, like a Greenwich Villager who had left her spectacles at home.

As she climbed down from the chair she tried to smile – failed miserably. She saw two of the girls exchange glances; noticed Marjorie's mouth curved in attenuated mockery – and that Warren's eyes were suddenly very cold.

'You see' – her words fell into an awkward pause – 'I've done it.'

'Yes, you've – done it,' admitted Warren.

'Do you like it?'

There was a half-hearted 'Sure' from two or three voices, another awkward pause, and then Marjorie turned swiftly and with serpent-like intensity to Warren.

'Would you mind running me down to the cleaners?' she asked. 'I've simply got to get a dress there before supper. Roberta's driving right home and she can take the others.'

Warren stared abstractedly at some infinite speck out the window. Then for an instant his eyes rested coldly on Bernice before they turned to Marjorie.

'Be glad to,' he said slowly.

## VI

Bernice did not fully realize the outrageous trap that had been set for her until she met her aunt's amazed glance just before dinner.

'Why, Bernice!'

'I've bobbed it, Aunt Josephine.'

'Why, child!'

'Do you like it?'

'Why, Ber-nice!'

'I suppose I've shocked you.'

'No, but what'll Mrs Deyo think tomorrow night? Bernice, you should have waited until after the Deyos' dance — you should have waited if you wanted to do that.'

'It was sudden, Aunt Josephine. Anyway, why does it matter to Mrs Deyo particularly?'

'Why, child,' cried Mrs Harvey, 'in her paper on "The Foibles of the Younger Generation" that she read at the last meeting of the Thursday Club she devoted fifteen minutes to bobbed hair. It's her pet abomination. And the dance is for you and Marjorie!'

'I'm sorry.'

'Oh, Bernice, what'll your mother say? She'll think I let you do it.'

'I'm sorry.'

Dinner was an agony. She had made a hasty attempt with a curling-iron, and burned her finger and much hair. She could see that her aunt was both worried and grieved, and her uncle kept saying, 'Well, I'll be darned!' over and over in a hurt and faintly hostile tone. And Marjorie sat very quietly, entrenched behind a faint smile, a faintly mocking smile.

Somehow she got through the evening. Three boys called; Marjorie disappeared with one of them, and Bernice made a listless unsuccessful attempt to entertain the two others – sighed thankfully as she climbed the stairs to her room at half past ten. What a day!

When she had undressed for the night the door opened and Marjorie came in.

'Bernice,' she said, 'I'm awfully sorry about the Deyo dance. I'll give you my word of honour I'd forgotten all about it.'

''Sall right,' said Bernice shortly. Standing before the mirror she passed her comb slowly through her short hair.

'I'll take you down-town tomorrow,' continued Marjorie, 'and the hairdresser'll fix it so you'll look slick. I didn't imagine you'd go through with it, I'm really mighty sorry.'

'Oh, 'sall right!'

'Still it's your last night, so I suppose it won't matter much.'

Then Bernice winced as Marjorie tossed her own hair over her shoulders and began to twist it slowly into two long blonde braids until in her cream-coloured négligé she looked like a delicate painting of some Saxon princess. Fascinated. Bernice watched the braids grow. Heavy and luxurious they were, moving under the supple fingers like restive snakes – and to Bernice remained this relic and the curling-iron and a tomorrow full of eyes. She could see G. Reece Stoddard, who liked her, assuming his Harvard manner and telling his dinner partner that Bernice shouldn't have been allowed to go to the movies so much; she could see Draycott Deyo exchanging glances with his mother and then being conscientiously charitable to her. But then perhaps by tomorrow Mrs Deyo would have heard the news; would send round an icy little note requesting that she fail to appear – and behind her back they would all laugh and know that Marjorie had made a fool of her; that her chance at beauty had been sacrificed to the jealous whim of a selfish girl. She sat down suddenly before the mirror, biting the inside of her cheek.

'I like it,' she said with an effort. 'I think it will be becoming.'

Marjorie smiled.

'It looks all right. For heaven's sake, don't let it worry you!'

'I won't.'

'Good night, Bernice.'

But as the door closed something snapped within Bernice. She sprang dynamically to her feet, clenching her hands, then swiftly and noiselessly crossed over to her bed and from underneath it dragged out her suitcase. Into it she tossed toilet articles and a change of clothing. Then she turned to her trunk and quickly dumped in two drawerfuls of lingerie and summer dresses. She moved quietly, but with deadly efficiency, and in three-quarters of an hour her trunk was locked and strapped and she was fully dressed in a becoming new travelling suit that Marjorie had helped her pick out.

Sitting down at her desk she wrote a short note to Mrs Harvey, in which she briefly outlined her reasons for going. She sealed it, addressed it, and laid it on her pillow. She glanced at her watch. The train left at one, and she knew that if she walked down to the Marborough Hotel two blocks away she could easily get a taxicab.

Suddenly she drew in her breath sharply and an expression flashed into her eyes that a practised character reader might have connected vaguely with the set look she had worn in the barber's chair – somehow a development of it. It was quite a new look for Bernice – and it carried consequences.

She went stealthily to the bureau, picked up an article that lay there, and turning out all the lights stood quietly until her eyes became accustomed to the darkness. Softly she pushed open the door to Marjorie's room. She heard the quiet, even breathing of an untroubled conscience asleep.

She was by the bedside now, very deliberate and calm. She acted swiftly. Bending over she found one of the braids of Marjorie's hair, followed it up with her hand to the point nearest the head, and then holding it a little slack so that the sleeper would feel no pull, she reached down with the shears and severed it. With the pigtail in her hand she held her breath. Marjorie had muttered something in her sleep. Bernice deftly amputated the other braid, paused for an instant, and then flitted swiftly and silently back to her own room.

Downstairs she opened the big front door, closed it carefully behind her, and feeling oddly happy and exuberant stepped off the porch into the moonlight, swinging her heavy grip like a shopping-bag. After a minute's brisk walk she discovered that her left hand still held the two blonde braids. She laughed unexpectedly – had to shut her mouth hard to keep from emitting an absolute peal. She was passing Warren's house now, and on the impulse she set down her baggage, and swinging the braids like pieces of rope flung them at the wooden porch, where they landed with a slight thud. She laughed again, no longer restraining herself.

'Huh!' she giggled wildly. 'Scalp the selfish thing!'

Then picking up her suitcase she set off at a half-run down the moonlit street.

# THE STORY OF PENGUIN CLASSICS

**Before 1946** ...'Classics' are mainly the domain of academics and students, without readable editions for everyone else. This all changes when a little-known classicist, E. V. Rieu, presents Penguin founder Allen Lane with the translation of Homer's Odyssey that he has been working on and reading to his wife Nelly in his spare time.

**1946** The Odyssey becomes the first Penguin Classic published, and promptly sells three million copies. Suddenly, classic books are no longer for the privileged few.

**1950s** Rieu, now series editor, turns to professional writers for the best modern, readable translations, including Dorothy L. Sayers's *Inferno* and Robert Graves's *The Twelve Caesars*, which revives the salacious original.

**1960s** 1961 sees the arrival of the Penguin Modern Classics, showcasing the best twentieth-century writers from around the world. Rieu retires in 1964, hailing the Penguin Classics list as 'the greatest educative force of the 20th century'.

**1970s** A new generation of translators arrives to swell the Penguin Classics ranks, and the list grows to encompass more philosophy, religion, science, history and politics.

**1980s** The Penguin American Library joins the Classics stable, with titles such as *The Last of the Mohicans* safeguarded. Penguin Classics now offers the most comprehensive library of world literature available.

**1990s** Penguin Popular Classics are launched, offering readers budget editions of the greatest works of literature. Penguin Audiobooks brings the classics to a listening audience for the first time, and in 1999 the launch of the Penguin Classics website takes them online to an ever larger global readership.

**The 21st Century** Penguin Classics are rejacketed for the first time in nearly twenty years. This world famous series now consists of more than 1,300 titles, making the widest range of the best books ever written available to millions – and constantly redefining the meaning of what makes a 'classic'.

**The Odyssey continues ...**

*The best books ever written*

PENGUIN 🐧 CLASSICS

SINCE 1946

Find out more at www.penguinclassics.com